Until the Big Water Takes Them

THOMAS -
  I AM IN YOUR
DEBT FOR THE GENEROUS
TESTIMONIAL. THANK YOU!

UNTIL THE BIG WATER TAKES THEM

ALWAYS,
JOHN JENSVOLD

John Jensvold

Until the Big Water Takes Them
Copyright © 2023 by John Jensvold

Paperback ISBN 978-1-959681-00-7
eBook ISBN: 978-1-959681-01-4
Hardcover ISBN: 978-1-959681-02-1

Library of Congress Number: 2022922015

Cover Image: Book Brush
Cover and Interior Design by Ann Aubitz
Published by Kirk House Publishers

Kirk House Publishers
1250 E 115th Street
Burnsville, MN 55337
612-781-2815
Kirkhousepublishers.com

The skylark flew within inches of the rocks
before it stopped and rose again.
The cost of flight is landing.

~Jim Harrison

PROLOGUE: MILLER'S LAKE

In its heyday, Dottie's Dock was the busiest lake marina in southern Minnesota. Its heavy timber T-shaped dock could tie down and protect as many as thirty fishing boats, a fleet of cruisers, and even a few pontoons. It was situated inside a recessed bay on the southern tip of Miller's Lake and the waves never seemed to survive the transition from the big water into the relatively calm interior of Budd Bay. The entrance to the bay was slightly offset, and the shores were lined with narrow pines and great oaks, gnarled and hardened by a century of life. In the 1950s and '60s, lake dwellers weren't so quick to remove trees; they much preferred to coexist with them, living in quaint cabins that abided the natural gaps. Most of those framed structures are now nearly extinct, along with so many of the magnificent trees. But in its heyday, if you didn't know the bay existed, you and your sleek Chris Craft with its chromed horn and whipping American Flag would simply pass by the well-cloaked entrance. Fortunately for Dottie's Dock, everyone knew exactly where it was.

The young boy was hot and sticky and dusty. It was a two-mile bike ride from his house on the other end of the lake to Dottie's Dock. On his first expedition to the place, he stupidly asked where Dottie was. The man behind the counter grimaced and informed the boy that Dottie had been dead for twenty-five years, and her husband too, almost as long. The place had been bought and sold several times since Dottie and Ralph started the business. It went under a couple of times, boarded up with the refrigerator and freezer turned off and emptied, only to be resuscitated again by a generous bank or a mawkish, romantic out-of-towner who knew the place's history.

"The Riegels own it now but they're never here. I think they live in South Carolina. Charleston, if you know where that is." The man said.

"Oh." The boy didn't have any clue where Charleston was located, or South Carolina for that matter.

"I don't mind you sitting in the bar at this time of day, but by lunch you need to be outside." The man was direct but not unfriendly. "What do you want?"

"Do you have any root beer?" the boy asked, feeling strange when the word beer came out of his twelve-year-old mouth. It seemed a little mysterious, maybe even treacherous.

"Yes! We have root beer, nice and cold for you." The

man pulled a frosty can out of the cooler and popped the top. "How about a beer glass for the root beer?"

"Yes please."

The boy was Owen Martin. He'd been adopted at ten years old by Sam and Samantha Martin, whose inability to have children was to remain a stubborn infection for them both, eventually ending their marriage. They argued incessantly prior to the adoption and even more vituperatively afterward. Samantha was appalled by the boy's given name and was astonished that the social workers would not support changing it to Vincent, her father's brother's name. He was too old, they insisted, at ten years, to assimilate a name change. It could be damaging and could very well lead to a collapse of the bonding experience altogether. Samantha openly complained that Owen was a weakling's name and that the boy would never outrun such a weakling's name. Samantha abandoned her new family while the ink dried on the paperwork.

On the bike ride home from Dottie's Dock, Owen grew concerned about the sudden narrowness of the gravel shoulder along the lake road. He hoped no large trucks would whir by and blast him with a wall of hot July air, sending him and his orange bike down into the ditch—or worse into a telephone pole. It seemed much farther going back home than it had on his way to Dottie's Dock. Or it may have been uneasy apprehension, knowing that it was Saturday and his adoptive father was off work and probably tinkering in the garage. Sam Martin was not vindictive or abusive by nature, but it seemed to Owen that he had lost interest in their murky relationship, with Samantha gone. Owen sensed that the adoption had been a final effort to reconcile a sickly marriage, and once the vaccine proved ineffective, it was basically discarded. With Sam Martin occupied in the garage, it would be a good day to hole up in his room and examine his coin collection, the sole possession that strung together several distinct episodes in his young life. Coins offered a tangible dose of permanence and calm that was otherwise unimaginable. Buffalo nickels were a personal favorite, and he was oddly encouraged by the Indian and the buffalo sharing the obverse and reverse of the same beautifully designed coin.

Sam Martin was indeed in the garage with the garage door open, and a box fan was plugged into the work bench, cranked to a noisy high. He acknowledged Owen with a crescent wrench salute and went back to the pesky carburetor on the lawn mower. Owen slipped inside his small room and dragged the cardboard box out of the closet that held his precious coins. He knew them all by heart, even though the collection now numbered 103. The house was a rental that Sam found when he took the job as an auto mechanic in the nearby town of Mercer. Owen had started school in Mercer, but there was just one month left before the summer break. Someone had left the questionable lawn mower in the garage.

At twelve, Owen knew he should have friends, but he didn't blame himself much because there just hadn't been opportunity. He laid out all of his coins on the low-pile carpet, taking care to arrange the coins in long rows by denomination. Wheat stalk pennies were on top, followed by his buffalo nickels, a few Mercury dimes, some silver Washington quarters that were all pre-1964, and one well-worn silver dollar—a Peace dollar from 1923 that had such an otherworldly look, Owen dreamed it had come from another planet. The silver dollar had been a gift from a social worker named Jenny at the last orphanage, and it had begun his obsession with coins.

Owen liked Miller's Lake and opened his window to catch the welcome breeze, which was laced with the pungent scent of algae that clung to the shore. It seemed like a very old and ancient smell that came up out of the earth from long ago. Owen thought of the dinosaurs.

The following Saturday morning, Owen was off down the road, peddling against a headwind, to buy a pop before lunch. The trip seemed much faster, and he considered that it was probably due to familiarity. The mile markers were all in place. The blue barn was the halfway point, and the fence made of repurposed wagon wheels was three-quarters. From that point, Owen caught his first view of the rooftop of the two-story wood-frame house that contained a small bar, lunch counter, and business office for Dottie's Dock. Rain had been scarce so far in July, and Budd Bay's water level was lower than normal, judging from the exposed water stains on the dock's support posts. The only boats moored were fishing boat rentals with numbers painted on the side and small outboards tilted up on the back ends. The four lonely boats bumped gently against the dock.

Owen went into the house and saw the familiar man behind the bar putting hot dogs on a heated roller with short tongs.

He turned to Owen. "You're back. Another hot one today. Hey, how old are you anyway?"

"Twelve."

"Twelve? Hmmm, well that's old enough to rent a fishing boat if your parents say it's okay. You know how to run a boat?" The man was half-serious, but more focused on the careful placement of each hot dog.

Owen ignored him. "What do you have besides root beer?" Owen asked.

"We got everything. Lemonade, Coke, Dr Pepper, let's see, Seven Up."

"I'll try a Seven Up." Owen spotted a curious panoramic black-and-white picture on the wall. It was a big gathering at Dottie's Dock with boats and people filling the dock and shoreline, all waving and saluting the camera. A large painted sign was held in the air by two girls that read "Happy 4th of July." Three young men stood together in dark sailor suits, with one showing his back to the camera. The letters spelled "Dottie's Deckhands." The dock and the surrounding small cabins were still recognizable but so much newer- and cleaner-looking in the picture, with well-pruned shrubbery and flags flying in the westerly summer breeze.

The man fetched a can from the cooler. "Those were the days. Twice you've been here now. What's your name? You live close by?"

"We live on the other end of the lake; it's a green cabin with a garage. My dad and I live there for his job. It's rented. I'm Owen Martin."

The man frowned slightly at the word "rented." "Well, good to meet you Owen. I'm Marvin, but everybody here calls me Marv. I run this place for the Riegels."

Later that week, a neighbor asked Sam Martin if his son would be willing to mow his lawn for twenty dollars. In a gesture that was uncharacteristic, Sam said he thought so and offered to gas up the repaired mower for Owen. Owen knew that twenty dollars would be enough for a second silver dollar, which he would acquire by mail from a coin dealer located in Mount Eden, Kentucky. The address was included in the back of a very dogged-eared coin magazine called *Numismatic Times*. Owen didn't know where Kentucky was either but figured it could be near South Carolina.

The next Saturday morning, it was less hot, with dozens of gauzy clouds drifting across a blue sky. The lake was dark in spots, where shadows shifted and teased the small waves in the big water. Owen was excited to see Marv and tell him about the silver dollar he had ordered. He would tell him about the whole collection if he showed enough interest.

Dottie's Dock was busier than usual, with six cars in the gravel lot and several new boats tied to the outer dock. Two young men came out of the house toting full minnow buckets and six packs of beer tucked under their arms. Owen wondered if Marv would let him take a barstool with such an unexpected level of commerce going on.

"Good morning Marv," Owen said with practiced good intentions.

"Hello there young man. Sit right here at the end," he gestured with his pinky finger to an empty stool at the end of the bar, right next to a chalkboard with scribbled rates for boat rentals, minnows, nightcrawlers, and leeches. Gasoline, too, was evidently available somewhere on the grounds, but Owen didn't know where.

"Whoa, you're busy today," Owen said, smiling.

"It's the weather. Perfect temp and a few clouds make the smallmouth bass come out of the reeds on the east side. My boats are all out," Marv thumbed enthusiastically through a wad of bills. "Are you fishing today? I've got plenty of bait."

Through the open windows, the murmur of boat motors gradually receded into the big water, giving room to hear the delightful calls of the red wing blackbirds flitting around statuesque blue herons. "No, I'm working on my coin collection today. I maybe will get a new silver dollar in the mail. At least I hope so."

"You're a coin collector? Very good. Everyone should have a hobby, I think. You know, there used to be a coin and antique shop not too far down the road. The building's still there. It started up right before Dottie and Ralph sold out. John Chambers owned the place; he still lives up the hill from the shop. He must be eighty years old by now. Maybe even ninety," Marv explained.

"Do you think he would talk to me about coins?" Owen was buoyed by the sound of "coin collector" and that it had been applied to him.

"I doubt it. He doesn't come down from that hill. Gets his groceries delivered from town. He's got a little contraption that pulls them up the hill. He's got an RV up there, a Winnebago I recall, but nobody is quite sure how he got the thing in place up there. It's quite a steep hill."

"Which direction is it?" Owen was persistent.

Marv rubbed his chin and stooped to look out the window and pointed. "It's on that gravel road, about a mile off the lake."

"Okay." Owen's gears were turning.

"Owen, I don't think it's a good idea to bother John Chambers. There was talk that years ago the shop got held up by two gangsters from Chicago and that he shot them both dead."

"Really? Did he go to jail?"

"No, that's the thing. The state police knew that two criminals were in the area around Miller's Lake. When gunshots were reported near Chambers's shop one night, the state police showed up before dawn to question John. Then they left. The shop was closed up the next day and soon after that John Chambers moved out of the back of the shop, up to the Winnebago he had moved to the top of the hill. People used to say that the police were just happy those Chicago boys were dead. John Chambers has been up there ever since. Must be forty years at least." Marv squinted at the floor, searching for more details. "Some people say that the two crooks are buried under that Winnebago. I guess we'll never know."

Owen examined Marv's face for some sign that he was playing a joke on him. There was nothing.

In bed that night, with the music of waves lapping against sand, Owen stared into the blackness of his bedroom ceiling and thought of John Chambers. It was easy to conjure an image of the coin and antique shop with its rooms in the back. Delicate turn-of-the century light fixtures dangled overhead with framed mirrors on the walls in all shapes and sizes. Carved wooden tables piled high with old gilded ash trays and bookends shaped like Egyptian Sphinxes. And long glass cases, well-lighted and holding a fortune in early American coins; gold and silver coins for sale or trade. Chambers was in bed himself, without doubt, when the midnight lock was snapped by thugs and, in a leaping instant, he did what he had always rehearsed in his mind. Grab the loaded pistol, point, and fire. And fire again, and again. There was no thinking called for and no fear of consequences. It was an instinct forged by repetition. Defend the shop. Or so Owen could imagine.

Another Saturday morning and Owen pedaled to Dottie's Dock. He paused at the entrance to the gravel lot. The mailbox had its red metal flag in the up position waiting for the mail truck. He looked to the right and saw the gravel road leading away from Miller's Lake, where, supposedly, a mile away was a treasure trove of coins and where one of the world's most renowned collectors resided in high security. Owen decided to forgo his can of pop and investigate John Chambers.

The overcast sky spit raindrops on Owen and he was grateful for the coolness they produced. The dusty road was easier to traverse with a little moisture to tamp it down. He saw the structure first; it was near the road, boxy and abandoned, shrouded by trees and wild brush. From the distance, Owen thought it looked like a crooked tombstone being eaten slowly by the Earth. His bike made a jerking sensation and the pedals locked. Owen stopped the bike and coasted to the grass. The chain had jumped off the sprocket and was firmly lodged alongside. If this was a potential catastrophe, he wondered, why did Sam Martin not warn him about it and what to do now? So many dangers lurk for a twelve-year-old. He left the bike and went on foot.

At about a hundred yards away, the faded sign was finally legible: "Chambers Coins & Antiques." The square building had windows on the front side, although none remained intact, and it was dry and weathered looking. There was a stub of a red brick chimney that had fallen over and left a few bricks scattered on the shallow sloped roof. On closer inspection, there was a side door that hung open, listless, relieved of its top hinge. Owen approached.

The shop seemed dead, deathly quiet and awaiting a burial. It gave off a foul odor that smelled like oil. Owen peered through a broken window and saw shattered glass and splintered wood, and he caught the unmistakable scent of vermin. There was a door leading to a room in the back, but Owen had no desire to explore any further. The whole building seemed ready to collapse. Around the side of the structure, there was a narrow path and it led to a small clearing. From there, Owen could plainly see the giant Winnebago perched on the top of a conical hill, with steep sides all around and a rickety cabled platform that seemed to connect the top to the bottom. Owen guessed that the Winnebago stood at least twenty feet above him. He thought about turning around and recovering his broken bike. He thought of Marv behind the counter at Dottie's Dock turning hot dogs with his tongs. He looked back at the forlorn, abandoned shop. He looked up at the Winnebago.

"Hello?" Owen shouted and then waited. "Mr. Chambers? Hello?" Owen was unnerved by the sound of his own loud voice in a place so silent.

There was no response.

"Hello? Mr. Chambers? Mr. Chambers?"

"Who in the hell is down there?" said John Chambers is a reedy, thin voice.

"Owen Martin. I'm a coin collector."

"I'm out of business. Go away God damn it."

Chambers's minatory directive tightened Owen's throat and made his still-developing voice absurdly high-pitched. "Mr. Chambers, I was hoping to ask a few questions about coins. Marv, down at Dottie's Dock. I mean, with your experience, I think I could learn some things from you. I only have a few magazines. I want to know if my collection is any good."

"What do you want to know?" The old man's tone leavened slightly but was still stern.

"I just thought we could talk a little about coins. My coins. I have one hundred and three with another one coming in the mail."

There was an awkward silence and Owen thought again about his crippled bike at the side of the road. *Is it still there?*

"What's on the reverse of a Franklin half dollar?" the old man croaked through the window of the Winnebago.

Owen immediately seized on his opportunity. "The Liberty Bell!"

"Get on the platform, push the button, and throw the lever," John Chambers instructed perfunctorily.

Owen eyed the platform. It was cobbled together with twisted gray lumber and rusty bolts, connected to a set of rails tacked into the steep incline, and with a loop of steel cable leading to a post and pulley on top of the hill. Owen thought about simply climbing the hill like a mountain goat, but he couldn't risk disobeying the old man and los-

John Jensvold ◆ 20

ing the opportunity to discuss coin collecting with an expert, an undeniable numismatic doyen. He climbed aboard, suffering a sliver in the heel of his hand, pushed the button with authority, and pulled the lever. A motor coughed and kicked into gear and the small platform began its ascent, remaining perfectly level along the way, and soon he could see the peak of the roof at Dottie's Dock.

As Owen approached the crest of the hill, he could see the old man in the window of the Winnebago. He looked sour and flinty.

"Push the button! Push the button!"

Owen panicked and began to grab at the lever, but checked himself, and pushed the button. The motor underneath the platform sputtered and hiccoughed to a stop. He had arrived at the precipice.

"Who the hell are you?" the old man squawked out the window.

"Owen Martin. I'm a coin collector."

"You look like a kid. I guess you can come on in." John Chambers expectorated into a tissue and wiped his mouth.

At one time, perhaps, the Winnebago had been an attractive avocado green with cream-colored stripes and forward-motion swirls. Now it was cast over with a dusty blanket of rust. The wheels were long since gone and the axles rested on concrete blocks. It didn't suggest sturdy in the least, but Owen opened the door anyway and climbed inside.

Owen pretended to ignore the offensive odor. Urine and human feces permeated the vehicle, which consisted of a smallish sitting area that had been hollowed out for a recliner and a large TV console. The walls and ceiling were lined with grainy wood panels that had a yellowish cast to them. A side table was taken over by stained coffee mugs and magazines. Owen noticed a bluish revolver on the shelf underneath, long-barreled with an ivory grip. The old man was the frailest human being Owen had ever seen in person. All bones. He had on pajamas and slippers, badly stained. John Chambers's mottled hands each gripped a cane and shook rather noticeably. Owen was relieved when the old man backed away from the window and dropped himself into the recliner.

"Listen," the old man recovered his voice, "before you ask your questions, how about dumping my bucket?"

"Bucket?" Owen was off balance.

"This one here, the orange one with the lid. Dump it outside past the funicular. Leave it out there to dry. It's stinking up the place terrible."

The price to play kept swelling, Owen thought, and his anticipated reward for exploring the unknown could rapidly dwindle to nothing. Still, where else should he be? He had no question about the contents of the bucket and he sure-handedly grabbed the handle. "What's a funicular?" Owen had no idea.

"A funicular, young man, is a cable car riding up the side of a mountain. I saw many when I lived in Switzerland and I built myself one when we set the Winnebago on top of Chambers's Mountain. You rode up on my funicular," John Chambers explained. "Dump the bucket."

The contents of the bucket had deliquesced to the point of syrupy goo, so outside he popped the lid and flipped it upside down on the ground and left it there. When Owen returned from the wretched task, he felt queasy and the stench hung in his nostrils. The old man had found the strength to open a folding chair in front of his recliner, and it looked safe enough. Owen appreciated the hospitality and sat down. It squeaked under his weight and that startled him.

"How did you start in the coin business?" Owen was assertive, trusting that the bucket dumping had earned him the right to ask a direct question.

"That was a long time ago and it was an easier business to get into. My lovely wife Doris and I traveled throughout Europe after the war; she accumulated fine antiques at cheap prices and I bought coins left and right. We shipped everything back to the States. We had a dream of opening a shop back home. In 1955, her cousin Dottie offered us a building she and her husband Ralph owned.

They started Dottie's Dock and it was the place to be back then."

"I heard," Owen said.

"People used to come from all over Wisconsin and Iowa and even Canada to Dottie's Dock. And they always wandered over to our shop. Doris and I were in heaven. After a couple of great years, though, we got robbed," the old man's voice trailed off in sadness.

Owen was reluctant to speak. Finally, he said "I heard you shot them."

"No. I didn't shoot anybody. They broke in at night and stole everything. The state police said that they probably had been watching us for a while. When they climbed back in their car, I did shoot at them a couple of times, but it was so dark, I don't think I came very close to hitting them. At least they didn't hurt us. But truth be told, the experience ruined my Doris and she never got over that night. Doris lost interest in the shop and her cousin Dottie tried to help, but Doris took her own life right down there at the shop. She swallowed all of her medicines at once. It was in the winter. That's when I bought the Winnebago and put it up here on the hill."

Owen struggled to contemplate the very nature of a violent robbery. It had always been an abstraction to him, like a TV drama. A fiction. But, inside the Winnebago with John Chambers, and with a crime scene just down the hill, the vicious act still possessed energy, and Owen felt his feet pinching with anxiety.

"Oh, dear Doris. Dear, sweet Doris." John Chambers stroked his temples.

"Is that the gun you shot at them?" Owen pointed to the shelf and wondered if it was loaded. It was resting so near to John Chambers. Owen glanced back at the door.

"What?" The old man dropped his chin to peer under his side table. "No, no. That's a fine specimen of a cap gun. Looks plenty real, though, I'll grant you that. Picked that up at a curio shop in Taos, New Mexico, one winter when Doris and I went that way antiquing. I use it to chase away a sanctimonious skunk who seems to think he owns the underside of the Winnebago."

"Can I touch it?" Owen asked curiously.

"No, better let it be."

"Okay."

"Let's talk about your coins now, because I have things to do," said John Chambers. "What do you have?"

Owen blushed and was instantly made self-conscious of the paucity of his meager cardboard box. "I have a lot of wheat stalk pennies and buffalo nickels. I have one silver dollar too, a Peace dollar. And I ordered a second one in the mail with the money I got for cutting a lawn. And I have three coin magazines, too. That's pretty much the collection, but it will grow." Owen tried to be precise.

"That is a very fine start." The old man gazed out the window as the raindrops grew larger and plunked away on the metal roof of the Winnebago. "You might get a little wet on your way home. You should head out, I guess."

"Maybe I can come back?" Owen asked.

"I am out of the business, as I said, but I have a gift for you, Mr. Owen, for coming all this way and having the courage to get on the funicular. They aren't doing anybody any good stuffed away up here on Chambers's Mountain, so better they go with you to goose the accelerator on your collection."

Owen didn't follow.

John Chambers fished around with his right hand in a large side pocket on the recliner. His hand emerged with a clear plastic cylinder, glowing with rich silver. "These were always my favorites." He handed it across to Owen.

It felt weighty in Owen's soft hands and he could see clearly the reeded edges of silver dollars stacked inside. "What are they?" Owen was certain that the old man was confused, or that he misunderstood. It most certainly couldn't be a gift.

"Morgans. All early ones. 1870s and 80s. There's twenty-five of them in there and they're all uncirculated. Works of art in my opinion. Damn fine coins. I never put those in the shop."

Owen held the cylinder delicately with both hands,

like he was handling a vial of plutonium. It made the old man grin.

"They're yours now," he announced rather proudly.

"Thank you so much, Mr. Chambers. I don't know what to say." Owen was filled with a new order of pride that seeped into his body from the plastic cylinder. He was infused with filaments of new responsibility, of ownership, of manliness, even.

"Next time you're down at Dottie's, see if there's a big black-and-white photo framed on the wall. It was the Fourth of July Boat Party in 1956. You will find me at the end of the dock. I'm the one wearing the stars and stripes top hat. That was a day. You get ahead of the rain now."

Owen reached out to shake the hand of John Chambers, but the old man was transfixed again by the window in the Winnebago, with a drained look of ineffable melancholy, so Owen left through the door quietly. He looked warily at the rickety funicular and decided it was safer to slide down the hill on his backside, digging in his heels for speed control.

He walked back toward Dottie's Dock and spotted his incapacitated orange bike lodged in the deep weeds. He looked back toward Chambers's Mountain and could see only the top of the rusted Winnebago. The funicular was buried behind the thick trees.

Back at Dottie's Dock, Owen asked Marv to look at his

bike, and in minutes, the chain was free and Owen was off, pedaling with one hand on the handlebar and the other nervously clutching the cylinder through his jeans pocket. Twenty-five uncirculated Morgan dollars, a veritable fortune, and he yearned to spread them all out on carpeted floor in his room. It would be safer to wait until his adoptive father was not at home. No chances could be taken with the Morgans. Owen was energized and optimistic as he cruised by the string of cabins and the blue barn halfway home. He imagined his biological parents smiling down at him as he carried his new treasure. For the first time, Owen experienced a deep urge to find them someday. He would show them his triumphant collection of coins.

Back on Chambers's Mountain there was a single gunshot that was heard by no one.

ONE

I hadn't been across the kitchen table from Ann Martini for fifteen minutes when the explosion shook the cabin. The shockwave tipped over a saltshaker, and the antique cuckoo clock on the wall crashed to the floor in a splintery thud. She stared at me, wide-eyed, paralyzed, frozen in place. Dust hung in the air and there was a ringing in my ears that was mildly painful. Instinctively, I went to the window thinking for certain a propane tank had ignited and burst. It was that loud.

"Holy Christ," I said, surveying the damage.

"Just tell me," Ann asked in an anxious whisper, still locked in place with her slim shoulders pulled in close.

"A huge boulder just took out one of your cabins. The ditch caught it before it got into the road. It's rocking back and forth. My God, never seen anything like that."

"Which cabin?" Ann was barely audible.

"The furthest one." I marveled at the destruction; a swath of flattened birch trees and shorn bushes yielded easily to the rampaging chunk of stone. It looked like a precision tornado had spun straight down the property's natural incline toward Highway 61. The boulder continued to expend its remaining energy, rocking back and forth in the ditch, much like a hissing and spitting locomotive that had stubbornly ground to a halt. It was squarish, the size of a commercial dumpster, copper-colored, and jagged in places. "I hope no one was in there." I looked back at Ann Martini. Still no movement from her.

"Go out there and look at it. Please—please, do it right now," she stuttered.

I went outside, and as I got closer to the scene, I slowed down and began inching my way forward, with trepidation. The wood-frame cabin had been literally sheared in half, cleanly, along the line of an interior bearing wall. An exposed bedroom and part of a living room and hallway were all that stood. A neatly made bed with silver sequined pillows looked serene and blissfully unaware of its close call. A framed picture hung above the bed on the rear wall, and it was comically cockeyed. From a distance, the picture looked like a lighthouse on a cliff, probably Split Rock, but it was hard to tell. A smear of twisted and snapped two-by-fours, mixed with spears of split lap siding and shredded asphalt shingles, formed a debris trail from the damaged cabin down to the road. I had seen enough violence in my life to half expect something horrific spread along in the debris, so I squinted defensively, scanning for any tell-tale signs of crimson. I carefully stepped around the mess, but there was nothing to suggest that anyone had been inside. The cabin was empty.

"Well?' Ann's voice quivered and she hesitantly stepped outside her cabin door with her gaze fixed firmly on her feet. She was about fifty yards away and I couldn't hear her well, but I understood.

"Nobody in here," I shouted back. It made sense that these more traditional cabins on the north shore of Lake Superior would be empty on a sunny, crisp afternoon in late April. It was prime weather for exploration and hiking. Rustic cabins like these were mostly for sleeping and morning coffee at a resort like Palisade Point. Still a lucky thing though. Nobody survives a rock like that one.

I walked back to Ann, who was now teary and red-faced. She turned away from me.

"You okay?" I offered softly, thinking that this girl may never have experienced a close shave with a dangerous, unbridled force that had no restraint or conscience. She looked terrified.

"I told you my sister Roxie and I own the Palisade." Ann turned back around to face me. "That's her cabin."

I understood the implication and glanced back at the damage. "Good thing she wasn't home. It's all okay now, except for your cabin, but anything can be fixed." I tried to be empathetic, but it was a weak suit for me given my predilection to keep emotional moments at arm's length. I suspected I sounded disingenuous, but Ann managed a stiff smile with damp eyes blinking.

"I never know where she is—she's not very dependable. She disappears a lot." Ann exhaled slowly and wiped her eyes with her sweatshirt, momentarily exposing a taut belly and a delicate navel that I couldn't help but notice. "Always been this way with Roxie." She carefully tucked her hair behind her small ears, revealing two little emerald studs set in gold.

Ann Martini was a petite flower with soft brown hair and a flawless complexion. She wore snug jeans that revealed nimble girlish legs. I could not envision her holding up under the coarse travails of running a resort in the Northwoods, especially through a winter. I, myself, have been adrift on the "resort circuit" for more than a decade. I knew firsthand that the summers demanded sweat and calluses that were rewarded by wood fires and night skies like no other. But winters were brutal and life altering if you ever dropped your guard—if you ever failed to think ahead and prepare. One look at the diminutive Ann Martini and I guessed there would be plenty of work for me at Palisade Point, no doubt in my mind.

Several cars had already pulled over and people were out milling around the angry-looking boulder and pointing up toward its probable origin. It was a towering Precambrian rhyolite curtain that dwarfed the modest collection of rental cabins called Palisade Point Resort. The State Highway Patrol arrived about twenty minutes later with flashing lights but no sirens. I caught sight of a white porcelain commode sitting upright on the shoulder of the road with its tank still somehow attached. A young boy excitedly tried to flush the oddity before being shooed away by his mother. A patrolman was talking people back into their cars, but a few lingered to take quick pictures. I learned years ago that falling rocks along Highway 61, also known as North Shore Drive, were commonplace once you were sixty or so miles up the coast from Duluth. That's where the monolithic outcroppings lined the winding lake highway all the way to Thunder Bay. By the way, Superior was no lake, at thirty-two thousand square miles, it was an icy sea with centuries of history swallowing ships and men, bordered by land that was only sporadically civilized.

"Maybe I should come back," I suggested to Ann Martini as the uniformed officers casually walked up the gravel driveway, glancing back at the boulder now resting peacefully in the ditch in a dissipating dust haze. I couldn't imagine it ever moving again. A curious squirrel explored the remnants of the far cabin.

"I think that would be a good idea," she said, wiping

her nose on her sleeve. "You can start tomorrow if you still want the job. What was your name again?"

"Owen Martin," I answered. "I'll see you tomorrow. I'm glad your sister's okay—I really am." I looked over at the wrecked cabin again and felt an unexpected twinge of loyalty to a young woman I had only just met. I had also just wasted my newest flannel shirt on a non-interview. She seemed like the type of person who would notice if I wore it again the next day and would be offended. I would have to consider my options, but that wouldn't take long since I was back living in my car, a Camry. I started back to my car but changed course to inspect the boulder. The expended energy still seemed present, palpable, like an aura. I patted the top and it was warm to the touch.

TWO

Aday earlier, I really had no plan other than to drive the North Shore. It was relatively palatable for me to live out of my car for short stretches, as I had done many times between gigs. My clean but rusted Camry had a dead odometer and unknown mileage that was on my mind lately. I was usually able to negotiate my way around car living during winter, but it had happened. Jobs were fewer during the low season on the resort circuit, so I generally asked for winter housing to be added into any deal for my summer services. The first order of business in the Northwoods is to be warm and dry through the winter months. Sometimes it just didn't work out and I occasionally froze my ass under blankets in the car with heat packs in my shoes, but for the most part I had avoided any prolonged suffering. Depending on the economy of the moment, most of the resort owners were desperate enough for competent help in the spring that they would promise just about anything to sign you up, including a free room for winter.

The back seat of the Camry was neatly packed with folded clothes, blankets, pillows and generally two or three books. My lack of formal education past high school was a nagging sore that I was committed to medicate at my own pace. I was nearing the end of a book about the survivalist Comanche Indians during the early Republic of Texas. It was a harsh part of our nation's history that I had known next to nothing about before stumbling onto this book. The Comanches were unrelentingly fearless for decades in the face of impossible odds against the well-equipped *taibo*, the White man. My other book was about the evolution of medieval armor. That one would probably have to wait for winter, after I studied the Comanches.

My trunk was filled with tools. I was more than a competent carpenter, drywaller, plumber, and electrician. Early in my life, I determined that if you didn't learn a skill yourself you couldn't guarantee the work, which equates to starvation where I'm from. It was that simple for me. My adoptive father's biggest contribution to my life had been a garage full of hammers, saws, socket sets, threaded pipe, lumber, and a couple of five-gallon buckets full of miscellaneous hardware—each piece a fascinating feat of engineering in its own right. He was gone a lot, and the loaded garage was my boyhood laboratory.

I was coming off a lucrative two-year gig in Bayfield,

Wisconsin, where I was part of a crew of three. The others were Louis and Tito, and we got along. We restored two Victorian-style stone houses for reuse as expensive bed and breakfasts. Built by the early Bayfield lumber barons in the 1880s, the houses were architectural gems but seriously water damaged and on the verge of collapse in some spots. The owner was willing to spring for exorbitant repairs, all on a time and materials basis with motel rooms just south of town included. He was looking to lure the big spenders who came up from Minneapolis and Chicago to sail tall double-masted schooners all summer long through the Apostle Islands. Madeline Island was the nearest to the coast and most prominent. We used to ferry over to Madeline on our off days to drink beer on the beach at Big Bay Town Park on the east side. On the two big Victorians, we had to do surgical excavations, replace foundations, rebuild roofs, completely replumb and rewire, then refurbish the interior finishes back to a near original condition, or at least historically acceptable. For restoration purposes, we referenced a set of very old sepia photos the owner had smartly collected, copied, and annotated with his own ideas and suggestions. Some of his notes were lifesavers, but some others were stupid, so we ignored them. He mounted the photos in a single album for our use. I liked the challenges of the work.

Halfway through demolition in one of the houses, I

discovered an original paneled pocket door sealed inside a pantry wall by later millwork modifications. Some long-gone craftsman was savvy enough to archive that door like a sealed time capsule rather than pop it out and truck it away to a landfill. It was original, pristine and with a patina that hearkened back to the day the first family moved into the mansion. I was proud to find a way to add the discovery back into our restoration work. After two years of steady progress, the three of us we were in sight of completion, but honestly the work had grown tedious for me, mostly because it was now all indoors. I was ready to move on from Bayfield. To where, I wasn't sure. I had accumulated enough in the bank to take my time with my next move.

I thought about the fact that I hadn't been on the North Shore of Superior for several years, and I missed the cleansing majesty of Superior, especially north of Two Harbors, where it got wilder and even hostile over the winter months. In Bayfield, the clustered Apostle Islands acted as a natural breakwater that tamed Superior sufficiently for sailboats. I longed for the untamed version and thanked my boss, who was fair with me, then headed back toward Duluth with a hankering for a return to the North Shore.

As soon as I got through Duluth and pointed the Camry north, help wanted signs popped up everywhere.

In Two Harbors you could begin to see the effects of corporate money taking over—something that I had heard about but hadn't really noticed firsthand. There was a time not long ago when the scattered array of littoral resorts and lodges were family-owned enterprises, with generational succession proudly proclaimed in the marketing brochures. North of Two Harbors, it looked to me like the few remaining traditional resorts clung to life on the land side of Highway 61. On the lake side, more extravagant resorts were gradually replacing teardowns. The big money wanted the spray of Superior on the windows of the super suites. It wasn't just the dichotomy of geography—land side versus lake side—the resort names gave it away too. Nearing Tofte, I passed by an erratically mowed parcel with three mismatched cabins (I guessed 1920s or '30s construction based on the squat design and small windows) with a solitary gas pump and a tire shop surrounded by stacks of old tires. A rusted tin sign read "Lloyd's Lodge & Service." A few miles further and across the road on the lake side was a sprawling four-story balconied hotel and a blocky indoor water park, all wrapped in expansive panels of blue-tinted glass with a Cape Cod theme. In the center of the complex stood a fifty-foot faux lighthouse. Hanging off the side of the lighthouse was a brass ship's bell suspended by a massive loop of rope that had likely never been to sea. A pylon sign with an electronic reader board announced in scrolling letters: "Welcome to the Blue Heron Retreat & Spa. Your Superior Adventure Awaits!" Both Lloyd's and the Blue Heron were hiring, but I felt uninspired for different reasons and kept driving.

A little further on, I drove by the modest Palisade Point Resort and was attracted to the careful symmetry of the dozen or so lap-sided cabins spread across a gentle rise of grass and trees with a massive rock backdrop. There were stone-ringed fire pits and painted picnic tables that brought images of happy families. The cabins were older structures like the ones I had seen at Lloyd's but far better maintained and painted a soft lemon yellow with white trim. Behind them lurked the namesake palisade, a towering rock outcropping that dwarfed the little buildings. The cabins had an air of noble defiance, which I admired, and maybe even some recklessness, sitting as they were beneath sheer rock that reached for the clouds. Here again was the ubiquitous "help wanted" sign that I had seen everywhere since Duluth. I passed two more newer resorts on the lake side and impulsively turned around and see what the opportunity looked like at Palisade Point. I could always say no if it wasn't to my liking. I turned in. The cabin nearest the entrance was the business office. There was a small black-and-white sign that said so. I parked the Camry, which shuddered to a concerning stop; it was overdue for service. I rapped on the front door, hoping for the manager.

She said her name was Ann Martini and invited me inside.

THREE

"Ed, you don't have to do this. Plenty of opportunity to unwind this plan of yours and you should think long and hard about Marie. Is this her decision as much as yours?" The banker, John Glendening, crossed his arms and sat back behind his maple desk.

"Of course it is," said Ed Martini.

"There's a lot more risk in this than you seem willing to acknowledge. Your finances. Your children. Your marriage. Long hours alone can't cure a diseased business. And Palisade Point doesn't make money. I can't say it any more plainly."

"John, I told you before, I worked twenty-three years to be *able* to do this. Preparation meets opportunity and that's Palisade Point. In my mind, I'm meant to buy the Palisade. Marie's on board and she full-well knows there's no guarantees. If we don't do this now, I have a feeling it will haunt us for the rest of our lives together," Ed Martini proclaimed, wearing a crisply pressed work shirt for the appointment with his longtime banker. He was resolute with a cautious smile, but he was not without trepidation at the prospect of so profound a life change. Despite his pronouncement, his wife Marie was not sleeping through the night, getting up at intervals for warm tea, and her extended family openly questioned why Ed would toss aside secure employment and a prospective pension for the muddy uncertainty of running a Northwoods resort. It didn't make sense to anyone other than Ed and Marie. Their young daughters were understandably nervous, but not afraid. Ed chafed under the undeserved criticism.

"Ed, the North Shore is a difficult place to raise two little girls. Ann's just a toddler."

Ed chuckled and laced his strong fingers. "Actually, I can't imagine a better place to raise our family. Wait and see."

Ed Martini and Marie Jacobson met as teenagers working as summer kitchen help at the historic Lutsen Lodge on Superior's North Shore. Marie waited tables and Ed washed dishes, generally, but on occasion they switched roles when Marie was suffering from hay fever and an embarrassing dripping nose. The young love they engendered during that first summer together was irreversibly imbued with the animal howl of crashing white caps under moon and stars. They were free to explore nature and each other. It suited them both perfectly. One day, they promised each other, they would return to Superior's shores and never leave. Ed was filled with pride and a pinch of jealousy when he overheard people at the Lutsen Lodge comment on Marie's remarkable beauty. Sometimes it was just a wink between men or an elbow nudge. She stood out against the rugged environment; there was no question about that.

They were married while still in their late teens, at Marie's family's church in nearby Hoyt Lakes. Her family liked Ed very much and knew he came from a long line of hard workers, honest people with an unflagging moral compass. Marie's parents had no reluctance to contribute their blessings to the union, despite their young age. Ed's family was less enthusiastic and had hopes that Ed would be the first of the Martini clan to go to college. The young couple moved in with Marie's parents, the Jacobson's, who were universally respected in Hoyt Lakes as a generous family who routinely took in people down on their luck. Partly to appease his family, Ed enrolled in classes at Hibbing State Junior College, deciding to become an electrician. This path seemed to satisfy everyone.

Ed graduated two years later as an apprentice electrician and was soon after employed full-time by the largest pit mining company on the Mesabi Range, called Kortech

Industries. The Mesabi Range was a hundred-mile ribbon of minerals stretching diagonally across northern Minnesota. Kortech went by several names during Ed's time with the company, with ownership changes getting more and more obfuscated over the years, leading to eventual rumors that it was no longer even an American company. The accepted legend was that Kortech was originally bankrolled by the Rockefellers at the dawn of the twentieth century. Ed never saw any real evidence of the Rockefeller's involvement, but he didn't see any reason to doubt it, either. So Kortech became Titan Industries, then United Solutions, and finally MHB, by then an ephemeral ghost of the original company, and it rendered Ed's soul empty. At that time, he began dreaming again of his magical summer with the captivating teenager Marie Jacobson at Lutsen Lodge and the electrifying discovery of sex, especially outside in the dark, with the full moon reflecting off Superior. They had found several favorite hideaways in the rock crevasses that lined the shore. Now, Ed's focus had changed forever. He was done working for others.

Under MHB's volatile management, most of Ed's close friends in the Electrical Services Department were unceremoniously dismissed and replaced by cheaper versions. Ed was on the younger side of the spectrum, but he knew the days were numbered. He saw lives literally torn asunder by the corrosive vices that afflict husbands and fathers who are suddenly cut off from income. He would never do that to Marie.

Early on at Kortech, Ed and Marie bought their first house in Hibbing, a modest bungalow with a stucco exterior, near the intersection of the leaf-covered streets Johnson and Van Buren. After more than two decades of service in a variety of electrical maintenance capacities, Ed was offered and immediately accepted a buy-out in 1994 when the "boom or bust" cycle of the taconite business had delivered another serious bout of anxiety for employees. He was weary, too, of the endless, nasty lawsuits that dogged every mining company related to environmental damage to his beloved Lake Superior. He felt fairly suffocated by his employer, so when the cash knocked, he took it without hesitation. Marie was fully occupied with her two high-energy daughters, just nine and three years old, but she had secretly worried about money for several years and what a job loss would mean for little Roxie and Annie. They had always been frugal, but savings never seemed to accumulate to the point of relief.

Banker John Glendening had known Ed Martini for much of his adult life. The men were close to the same age and fellow third-generation immigrants. John was a teller at Station Bank in Hibbing on the day Ed strolled into the bank lobby with his first modest bonus check from Kortech in hand. Over the years, John's banking career gained steam as he ascended the ranks, from branch manager to vice president and, finally, to senior vice president with the sole authority to grant the loan Ed requested, to close on the Palisade Point Resort in Tofte, Minnesota. The Palisade. With its smattering of dilapidated cabins situated across the road from Superior, the rising topography of the property fortunately gave them all an unimpeded view of the big water. John Glendening reluctantly acquiesced to the loan, but it didn't pass muster with him. Nowhere near.

Ed and Marie Martini took possession of Palisade Point in March of 1994 and found the buildings to be in worse condition than expected. There was rot in several of the roofs and undersized floor joists resulted in bowed floors. Still, Ed assessed there was much to salvage and improvements could be made rather quickly. There were six cabins placed somewhat haphazardly across the inclined parcel. Scrub trees and buckthorn were everywhere, untended for years. They committed to the tasks of renovating, expanding, and winterizing the cabin closest to the road that would serve as home, and the nerve center for Palisade Point. Cash leftover from the down payment was limited and precious. Ed would gradually renovate the rest, one at a time, starting with the one in the worst condition, using reclaimed materials he bought off his neighbors. His sheaf of penciled spreadsheets of revenues and expenses had been revised so many times there were annoying eraser-rubbed holes in important places. All of Ed's business scenarios made one thing crystal clear and validated John Glendening's misgivings. More cabins would have to be added, sooner than later, to make Palisade cash flow. He kept his thoughts at that time to himself, protecting Marie from uncertainty. Ed reckoned he would need an oversized garage for equipment, tools and materials, too. He set to work, picturing John Glendening watching over him with benevolent suspicion.

After so many years in round-the-clock mining operations, Ed was used to long hours, which served him well as he and Marie worked side-by-side on their cottage and garage projects while tending to the first few paying customers of spring. Marie hoped for faster progress, fueled by her constant worry over money and her emerging concern over the girls' isolation at the resort.

Ed was meticulous by nature, with a "measure twice and cut once" mentality that was reinforced by his electrical training. Marie was a novice at building improvements but proved herself adept with scrapers and paintbrushes and could work just as hard as her husband, despite her diminutive frame and small hands. There was talk of a new resort planned on the lakefront nearby that was rumored to include over two hundred guest rooms. Ed couldn't fathom how such a massive investment like that would ever pan out in tiny Tofte. It just wasn't possible.

Ed Martini left John Glendening's office with the signed loan agreement he had promised his wife Marie. Ed realized that without his friend's approval, the entire adventure on Superior would have ended abruptly with no way forward. Glendening's female assistant slipped into Glendenning's spacious office as soon as Ed walked out the front door of Station Bank and Trust.

"Another satisfied customer?" she asked nonchalantly, secretly wishing her boss was younger.

"There goes a man with a fair measure of perspicacity." Glendening shrugged and went to the window.

"Translation please?"

"Ed Martini is not prone to making mistakes, even though it might appear he's stepping into quicksand."

"Shrewd?"

"Yes. That's a good word for him. And I'm counting on that quality more than his business plan, frankly."

FOUR

O n my way from Duluth to Tofte, I remembered seeing a small wood-frame building in the town of Schroeder that offered gas and groceries. There wasn't a sign anywhere on the building, but the windows were plastered full of hand-drawn signs blaring specials on cigarettes and sliced meats. I found it right where I remembered and pulled in because it had the unmistakable look of a sole proprietorship. I learned from experience that such owners were more inclined to let people like me park for the night, especially if I set a twenty on the counter. It was an unadvertised part of the business. The franchise chains have rules against itinerant laborers like me sleeping overnight in their parking lots. I didn't take it personally. I inquired inside and placed a folded bill on the counter. The gray-haired man behind the counter wore a red and black checkered flannel shirt. He patted the twenty and grinned knowingly, raised an eyebrow, and shook his head in the affirmative. Then he gestured toward the backside of the graveled area along-side the store, and I nodded. The deal was made. He then generously poured me a free medium coffee, which was unexpected and appreciated. I had the distinct feeling that the manager had overnighted in a few parking lots himself in his day. I thanked him and took a look around the store, sipping my steaming coffee, which the man proudly an-nounced was a new hazelnut flavor. In the back of the place, there was a large refrigerator with pop, milk, cheese, sliced meats, and translucent plastic buckets of pickled herring. Next to the refrigerator there were four rows of shelves with all kinds of dry goods. In the corner I discovered a bubbling water tank full of twitching min-nows. Circling back to the front, I found the ubiquitous rotisserie of dirty magazines: *Playboy*, *Hustler*, and one I didn't recognize called *Farm Girls*. A sign behind the man-ager offered fishing licenses and lottery tickets. I spotted a map of the Temperance River trails that snake upland from Lake Superior into the Sawtooth Mountains and de-cided to buy it. I was already thinking ahead to a glorious day of hiking upland in one of my favorite parts of the world. It had been so long.

The next morning, I turned into Palisade Point around nine and got my first glimpse of the sister, Roxie. She was poking around the damage to her cabin and then she turned and disappeared into the adjacent garage. I waited

in my car, unsure of whether I should walk over to introduce myself or find Ann. Roxie returned with a rolled-up
blue tarp tied in the middle with a white cord. At a distance, Roxie didn't look much like her sister. She was taller
and darker, with long black hair woven into a ponytail
that had a little red bow at the bottom. It swung back and
forth as she walked like a waggling fishing lure. She had
an athletic build, graceful, and moved with purpose.

Ann came to the screen door and suggested we sit
down at the picnic table to talk. She talked fast and was
clearly still upset about the incident with the boulder, but
gradually she calmed down. She went over the basics for
Palisade Point, how it runs, a little about her family, and
we agreed on a monthly stipend to mow the grounds,
clean the grills, split and distribute firewood to the cabins,
some painting and repairs from time to time, clean toilets
before every reservation, and generally be on-call six days
a week. I could have Mondays off, although that wasn't
written in stone, she said. She asked if I could help do
something with Roxie's wrecked cabin and I agreed to
help with that too. Ann said Roxie may stay with a friend
for a while.

I resisted the temptation to compute the hourly com-
pensation because the more she talked the lower it fell. I
guessed it didn't really matter since my bank account was
thicker than usual, and outdoor work was very appealing.

There is no better place to spend a summer than the North Shore, and she said I could stay free through the winter, although she would only pay me through September. I was in dire need of physical exhaustion, which was the salve that kept me from thinking too much about myself.

"Which cabin do you want me to take?" I asked, watching Roxie roll out the blue tarp.

"Owen, we only have eleven. Roxie's is Number Eleven, and I'm here in Number One. You get the second bedroom in mine. It's not big, but you have a door at least."

"With you? You're comfortable with that?" I was wary, especially around attractive women. I sensed a trap, and I had a talent for dodging sucker punches.

"You have a problem sharing my house?" Ann was playful but serious.

"Well," I was slightly off balance. "What if I snore?" *What a moronic question.*

"I snore, too, like a fucking lumberjack," she proudly declared, clearly satisfied by the tone of her own expletive.

I scratched at the back of my head, an old childhood habit to expedite decision-making under duress. "Okay, I suppose it's fine, if you're okay with it."

Her smirk vanished and brought narrowed eyes. "Please take a good look at my bathroom Owen. It's clean for a reason. That's my only rule. Do whatever you want in your bedroom."

Ann awkwardly shook my hand with both of hers and went back inside. How could her hands stay so impossibly soft in this wilderness? I meandered to my car, still a bit stunned by the sleeping arrangements. I immediately imagined all sorts of embarrassing predicaments I could fall into, but I was energized, although thoroughly uncomfortable. Not since a pretty girl in Green Bay lifted my wallet at a saloon after a night of drinking had I felt so entirely laid bare, exposed. I soothed my anxieties with the knowledge that I would always have car keys tucked in my pocket and could simply fire up the Camry and drive away if things went off the rails. It was the very nature of these jobs anyway. Always unorthodox in one way or another. At the core I was a tool-wielding mercenary with a bed promised for winter.

I suppose my lingering fear of robbery since the Green Bay incident led to my habit of regularly popping my trunk to check on my tools. A quick visual inventory cleared my mind and relaxed me. I opened up the backseat to toss together a duffel with toiletries and a few changes of clothes that I had layered on the car floor. I thought of bar soap but couldn't seem to find any in the various pockets I stowed them. My chunk of soap always grabbed a residual hair or two and dried it into place for next time. That wouldn't do with Ann, clearly. My bathrooms trips would need to be invisible, stealthy, completely portable and evidence-free. Private provisions would be needed right away. I shut the car door and turned to find Roxie standing right behind me without sound or warning. She was nearly my height and fixed to the ground like an oak tree. I felt my face flush and a claustrophobic heat net dropped on me and made my toes curl in my shoes. Likely it had been presumptuous on my part to accept the job before meeting Roxie. If Roxie was pissed off, how could I really blame her?

"Just for the record," Roxie started off, sternly eyeing me up and down, "Ann's the one who thinks we need help."

"You must be Roxie. I'm Owen Martin."

"I know who you are." Roxie inched still closer.

I would have backstepped in response but was already up against the Camry. I tried to quickly evaluate her expression and posture. She gave away no clues other than fearlessness, with smooth caramel skin, high cheekbones, and a canine focus. "You have a beautiful place here," I responded, "I'm looking forward to helping you both out, whatever you need me to do. I'll just drop this bag inside. I'm on the clock, so to speak. I'm all yours." I stuttered slightly and didn't care for it.

"You need to get up to Grand Marais and pick up a

kayak we bought. There's a travel rack in the garage over there that straps onto your car."

"Straps to my car?"

"Crack your windows and feed it through. Get it nice and tight or you've got problems." Roxie handed me a scrap of paper. "This is his address. It's near the start of the Gunflint. Keep driving until you see signs. His name's Ned Nielsen. He's tall and bald with a gray beard. It's paid for so don't let him charge you for anything else. He likes to add things to the bill, especially if he doesn't know you."

"Okay, I can do that." It was not exactly the day one I envisioned when I shook the tender hands of the delicate Ann Martini, but an hour drive north along Superior sounded very welcome in current circumstances.

"There's gas in the red tank behind the garage and a five-gallon can inside somewhere. That's enough to get you there and back. Don't let anything happen to the kayak; it's almost new, and it's yellow. Don't let him give you the wrong one. I've got a cave tour on Friday and I'm short one kayak. I get a hundred bucks a person."

"Sure thing. I'll get going right now." I was already sequencing the tasks in my head, glancing toward the big garage, picturing a cylindrical tank elevated up on steel legs, finding the five-gallon can, and then, regrettably, envisioning a yellow kayak airborne and flying high and free over Highway 61 in a day one debacle of epic proportion. If that happened, I'd just keep driving.

"One more thing, Owen Martin. Don't ever convince yourself that it would be a good idea to try to get in my pants. That goes for Ann too."

FIVE

I was plenty relieved to arrive back at Palisade Point with the yellow kayak still clinging to the roof of my Camry, after one close call just out of Grand Marais that stopped my heart. The tie-down rack Roxie provided might have worked well in in theory, but it was lousy in practice since the straps loosened up whenever a gust of wind got underneath. I hung on to the edge of the kayak's cockpit with my outstretched left arm the whole way back. My left shoulder started cramping like a demon halfway as I breezed by Lutsen. Three-quarters of the way the pain intensified to the point where my eyes watered, clouding my vision. I distracted myself with random thoughts. It occurred to me that I should have left my packed duffel in the backseat of the Camry. That way, when I lost the kayak, I could just keep driving without abandoning my gear. That was an obvious oversight. It was a sobering enough exercise to momentarily distract from the shooting shocks up and down my flexed arm. As I said, the kayak and I both arrived intact, except for a sore shoulder that wasn't much cause for long-term concern.

"Took you long enough," Roxie commented, coming out of the garage wearing work gloves and bib overalls with a long-sleeved football jersey underneath. She was square-shouldered, and her even tan was no doubt the result of kayaking in the early season sun, with powerful reflection off the surface of Superior's back channels.

"I had some trouble with the rack."

"It looks okay," Roxie surmised, making a circular inspection. "Thanks for picking it up. I made room for it next to the others. Nielsen ask you for anything?" Roxie was less abrupt with me and I sensed that maybe my delivery built up a little capital with her.

"He wasn't there. I talked to his wife. She was very nice."

While I was gone Roxie had finished stapling the blue tarp to the edges of the gaping wound to her cabin.

I looked it over. "Did you sleep in there last night? No power or water?"

"Where else would I sleep? I used the bathroom in Number Ten. We need to get this place repaired ASAP. The foundation barely got touched, just a couple of loose concrete blocks. I need you to clean this up and see if you can reclaim any of the wood. There must be something."

"Do we burn what's left over?" I asked, concerned

about the dry spring. We were surrounded by forest, after all, but it was usually the cheapest way to dispose of construction debris.

"Burn what you can, carefully. Cut some of it up for kindling and tie a bundle for the cabins. Folks will use it up quick. There's a dumpster behind the hardware store in Schroeder. I've brought trash there after dark."

"I bet they appreciate that." I said, attempting levity.

Roxie stared back at me quizzically, as if I spoke a foreign language.

"Sounds like a plan," I said. Admittedly, I was drawn to her defiant attitude. That was my way too, but I didn't announce it to the world like she did.

"When you're done with that, make a list of materials we need to put my cabin back exactly the way it was. You claim to be a carpenter, so how long you need to reframe it?"

"I, I suppose, once we get the lumber here, maybe, a week?"

"Can't be any longer, Owen. We will be filled up by the end of May. I need my cabin back with a bathroom. Besides, there's lots of other work to do, too." Roxie pumped three more staples into the tarp in rapid succession, pulling it taut as she went along.

"I guess maybe you *do* need me after all."

Roxie glared at me, then returned to stapling.

I questioned the structural integrity of the remaining cabin after being sheared in half by a tumbling boulder. How could half of the building survive the impact of two-ton rock rolling downhill at thirty miles per hour? Roxie stopped to watch me thinking. She must have picked up on my thoughts because she informed me that Number Eleven was one of the cabins her father Ed had built himself, ground up, right after he and Marie bought Palisade Point. Roxie called it a "real brick shithouse."

Later, Roxie got in her VW bug and took off south on North Shore Drive. I watched her until she disappeared around the first bend. She reminded me of a couple of people I had worked alongside in construction over the years and, oddly enough, both were men. Roxie was just as physically riveting as Ann, but in an entirely different way. I felt a tugging responsibility to protect Ann. With Roxie, I felt a nascent survival instinct bubbling up inside.

It took just three hours to cut and stack up the shattered remains of the cabin. Not much of it had any chance of reclamation, but I salvaged a few two-by-fours to demonstrate a good-faith effort. I bagged up the torn shingles and tar paper and carpet and glass shards, thinking about the dumpster at the Schroeder hardware store and picturing the owner waiting in the weeds with a loaded twenty gauge. I counted twenty-two filled bags. The debris removal would take a month if I wanted to stay inconspicuous and drop two at a time and skedaddle. Maybe I could offer the guy a hundred out of my own pocket to let me dump it all in the daylight? No, too much money, and anyway, I thought I might get a rush from being in cahoots with Roxie Martini. I took down part of the tarp to inspect the edges. Other than badly mangled water and sewer piping and a dozen dangling wires, it was a relatively clean line of destruction. I retrieved a pad and pencil from the Camry and, with an experienced hand, drew out the design details I would need to make a decent materials order.

It's hard to break a sweat on the North Shore in chilly April, but as soon as I finished the clean-up, my damp back turned cool and stiffened enough to make me groan. I saw Ann come outside to sit at the picnic table in front of Number One. It looked like lunch was served. I got closer and could see we were about to share turkey sandwiches with lettuce on white, all cut with caring precision into quarters. There was a clear glass pitcher filled to the brim with iced lemonade, and thin slices of lemon and lime behaved like butterflies as she stirred the mixture. The plates were a cobalt blue and contrasted boldly against the white table. I tried to recall the last time someone served me lunch, but nothing came to mind.

"I saw Roxie head south in her VW," I said, not thinking any more about it.

Ann strained to look down Highway 61. "She's probably headed to Duluth. She has a friend there, Caprice Wind. She's an Indian. Fond du Lac Chippewa."

"Sure," I answered, more interested in my sandwich than Roxie's plans, since there was a tangy mustard of some sort that was delicious against the lemonade. The waves on Superior were rising and I detected airborne mist from the white caps on my face, which of course was not possible at that distance.

Ann giggled at me. "Roxie's gay, Owen. Caprice is her girlfriend."

I gathered myself, feeling the full weight of Ann's attention on me. "Well, Roxie's a very beautiful woman and I'm probably not the only one who thinks so." I stammered a bit but thought I recovered sufficiently. I didn't know anything about gay people and wasn't certain if I had ever met one, *although who knows*?

"People who know them both think they're the sisters, not me and Roxie." Ann added with a hint of sadness that didn't last long. "Have another sandwich, Owen."

"I believe I will." They were fresh and delicious.

"Caprice's family doesn't like Roxie much. They think she's responsible for Caprice's orientation. Have you ever heard of such lame-ass thinking as that? Like it's contagious or something?"

"How old is Roxie, anyway?" It was a clumsy attempt to shift to safer subject matter.

"Thirty-six last August," Ann answered nonchalantly, then paused and looked up at me. "How old do you think I am?' She was coy and reveled in my helpless expression.

"Younger?"

"Good answer. Kind of a pussyfoot answer, but pretty nimble since I just made you lunch."

"Thanks."

"I turned thirty in February."

"Okay." Honestly, I would have guessed younger than that, if pressed. There was a flirty girlishness to Ann that suddenly made me feel queasy about the shared accommodations. I needed to get back to work before she started asking me questions about myself. Questions that I detested to answer.

"Sandwiches and lemonade were incredible, Ann. I can't remember a better lunch. But I have work to do."

"Fine by me." Ann deftly gathered up the dishes and glassware onto a tray and toted it felicitously back into Number One.

SIX

I worked straight through the first ten days to establish a baseline of credibility with Roxie and to exhaust myself enough to resist sitting around the night sky fire with Ann, despite her invitations. I hadn't been with a woman in months, and the combination of her feline movements and mischievous eyes, mixed with what surely would be a full glass of red wine in my hand, suggested I take certain precautions in my new life. We were fast approaching the middle of May and six of the rentable cabins would be filled from Thursday through Sunday. Most were young families who, according to Ann, yearned for early season hikes up the stony Temperance River after being cooped up all winter with little Willie and Nellie down in the Twin Cities. There was also one solitary and accomplished author who visited Palisade Point every spring, Roxie told me, almost as a warning. She said that he had stopped writing years ago when Parkinson's ushered in a new phase of his life, but he came back every year, perhaps drawn by nostalgia, and always requested cabin Number Five, where his deceased wife had joined him many times. His name was Baskins, she said. I had never heard of Baskins but hoped we might have a conversation if an opportunity presented, despite Roxie's cautions. One night when I decided finally to join her at the fire, Ann shared that in May they begin the humbling process of refilling the bottomless money bucket that provides oxygen to the resort. She seemed melancholy at the prospect and I stayed silent.

It was Wednesday, my chores were done for the most part, and Ann was busy baking cinnamon-laced sweet bread. Roxie had yet to return from her rendezvous with Caprice Wind in Duluth. I asked Ann if Roxie was overdue. She complained that it did no good to settle on timeframes with Roxie as they were never abided anyway. Suddenly unencumbered by pressing work obligations, although cabin Number Eleven was incomplete, it seemed like a day off beckoned and Ann said it was fine for me to go. I truly hoped I would meet Caprice Wind someday. Whoever was able to captivate Roxie Martini was worth meeting. I stopped myself short before imagining Roxie and Caprice together romantically in Duluth. That was supremely difficult to do.

There was a paved trail on the lake side of the Highway 61 and I jumped across to begin walking south, or really southwest, given the rugged slant of the North Shore. After a couple of hundred yards, I began to see the white and gray colors of the massive Blue Heron resort peeking through the thick spruce and the thick blanket of bright green sumac. I thought it worthwhile to make a closer inspection since building structures of all sorts intrigued me immensely. After all, I had no schedule, for one day at least, and the breeze off Superior was enlivening to the point of fine perfume, laced with pungent evergreen. The day started sunny but had turned grayish by midmorning, and Superior had gradually given up its brilliant blue for dull hues. The big lake was never the same sea twice; it was constantly changing and becoming. I zipped up my jacket. We were still a good month out from summer weather at this latitude.

Strolling lazily along the trail toward the Blue Heron afforded me a gradual appreciation of the sheer size of the complex, with its many interconnected boxes and towers. There was much that I had not seen when I first drove by in the Camry. First of all, to assemble such a large parcel along the shore, I could envision four or five teardowns of resorts like the Palisade must have been necessary to simply consolidate the site. The teardowns would have been family cabins, traditional resorts, maybe motels, or some combination of the three. The fact remained that those little histories, those family stories, were lost, imploded, just like the people who gave them life, all dying for the sake of a massive corporate investment by impersonal money. I was biased against big business because I felt it was biased against me.

As the Heron came into clearer view, I could plainly see that it took up at least a thousand feet of lake frontage; the shoreline was mostly weathered shelves of prehistoric rock that formed a massive promontory. The shoreline persisted resiliently against eons of rolling white surf. It was the only line of defense between the oblivious people inside the Blue Heron and the big lake hoping to lap them up unawares. It was obvious to me that the Blue Heron was designed to maximize the water's edge, with the most profitable units, the fancy ones, nudging the recreational amenities, shops, and cheaper lodging further back into the interior of the site. None of that was surprising. The life-size faux lighthouse was fully equipped with a perfunctory beacon that, instead of warning away endangered ore ships, announced Happy Hour. That was what the sign said. It looked much bigger in person than it had from the highway. The water park was filled with bright jumping colors and arms and legs flying in every direction. There was a steady hum of melded shrieks emanating from the glass and steel box.

Finally inside the main entrance, I sought out the bar,

as was my custom in any new environment. If you want to learn about a place, find a bartender. The Blue Heron had two such oases. One was a contemporary lounge with a piano player that commingled with an upscale restaurant called Fortunes, and the other was next door and it looked to be an effectively contrived Irish pub. It was called Keegan's and more my speed. What lengths places will go to pretend to be what they're not. The presumption that there ever was an Irishman in charge named Keegan was dubious at best. It had dark wood, which I admired, and crimson and green plaid carpeting. Convincing electric reproductions of gaslights flickered overhead. Keegan's was boiling with activity and the pressed tin ceiling amplified the din, but the heavy-set balding bartender was assured and instantly likable. I could easily pretend that I had inadvertently stepped onto a movie set at the old Warner Brothers studios. There was a life-size statue of James Cagney standing in the corner wearing a kilt and a menacing half scowl.

"Welcome to Keegan's. What can I get you?" the thick man behind the bar asked jovially above the rising noise.

"I suppose a scotch or whiskey is in order here."

"Indeed. We have everything."

I concluded that in a solo celebration of my new job at Palisade, whatever it would become, and my equal doses of attraction and trepidation where it concerned the Martini girls, the fact that I had a stiff, folded fifty emboldened me. "I'll have a Balvenie. Neat. Do you have a Doublewood twelve?" I inquired as I visually perused the long row of backlighted bottles of amber delights. It brought me back to Dottie's Dock, a decrepit lakeside bar I illegally frequented as a young boy, ordering soda pop alongside morning drinkers.

"Friend, why don't you treat yourself to a Portwood twenty-one? I just uncorked it and had a sniff myself. Magnificent. The best thing to come out of Scotland since William Wallace."

"That much the better, huh?" I was uncharacteristically inclined to jump the two shelves.

"You be the judge." The balding man gave me a hearty handshake with a bear hand and mentioned that he was a retired pipefitter from Ely, and that his name was Dean.

I nodded approval and Dean the bartender spun into motion, reaching and grabbing and pouring, until finally producing a short crystal tumbler that was heavy at the bottom and sparkled around the rim like a halo of cut diamonds. I stared at the shimmering amber liquid awhile, remembering that this was basically how Nostradamus predicted the future. I sipped at it tentatively. Portwood 21 had a remarkable flavor, different from my recollections of the more oaky Doublewood. It was a more complicated flavor, changing from the lips to the tongue, a preserved remnant of a time long gone, with a nuanced smoky sweet aftertaste that was agreeable to my middle. The planet that had produced this Portwood 21 was changed today, but here was its history in my glass. After another measured sip, my joints loosened and the nagging cramp residing in my left shoulder dissipated altogether. All my life I have cherished little unexpected pleasures garnered in unexpected places. Keegan's continues the queue. Like finding a silver dollar buried in the sand.

"So, are you just getting in?" Dean asked, clearly pleased with his timely liquor recommendation and another successful up-sell.

"No, just taking a look around the Blue Heron. I started work at Palisade Point."

"For the Martinis?"

"Ann and Roxie. My name's Owen."

"Well, I don't know the young ladies. I knew Ed for twenty years when we were both in the trades. He was an electrician and worked for one of the big boys over on the Mesabi. Good people. I miss seeing Ed and Marie around here. They were some of the originals. Not many left from that generation. It gets harder and harder to survive."

"Ed and Marie, are they still with us?" I asked gingerly, never too confident with such a prying question, but

I was genuinely curious about the family history, and neither Ann nor Roxie had mentioned anything about their parents—it hadn't been my place or the time to ask. "Marie's gone some years now, I recall, but I think Ed's still languishing in a nursing home down in Duluth, at least I haven't heard that he has passed. He had a stroke a few years ago. I remember seeing an ambulance at Palisade Point on my way to work one day. I thought about stopping but kept driving. The news got around fast and that was a sad day." Dean paused to collect himself. "So, after that happened the daughters took over. How are they doing, anyway? Seems like an awful lot for two young ladies, especially with all the new competition. Just look at this place." Dean extended his burly arms and spun himself completely around on one foot, as confident as a compere centered on a Vaudevillian stage. "We've got a hundred and eighty suites all on the water's edge. Those girls must know their onions for keeping a Mom and Pop running up here these days. Care for another Balvenie Mister Owen?"

"Better take it down a shelf," I said and took a last look at my crisp fifty. I noticed Dean's gaze had fixed upon the passing backside of a young woman in snug white shorts with floral panties showing through. He shook his head wistfully and resumed my pour.

"I like women," Dean announced proudly. "All

shapes and sizes, doesn't matter a whit to me. And up here they all seem to pass through Keegan's eventually. I just have to keep my eyes peeled."

"I presume they return your affections?" I joked.

"Not very often anymore, but I'll die trying." Dean laughed out loud and banged on the cash register, making it sing.

Outside I forged a somewhat circuitous path around and through the multitude of buildings that comprised the Blue Heron. The water park was an enormous barn-like building covered in glass. From outside I saw hordes of screaming wet kids ascending a four-story stairway to the top of the giant corkscrew slide. How odd to drive the family two hundred miles to the edge of the greatest fresh-water lake in the world, and then choose instead to splash away indoors a stone's throw from Superior. It was incomprehensible to me, but safety reigns these days, and there was nothing safe about Superior.

I took the paved trail back toward modest Palisade Point. About halfway home I saw Roxie out in front talking to a taller man who was standing next to a shiny pickup truck. After another fifty yards I could discern the Cook County logo on the truck's door. There were six or seven cars parked alongside the looping gravel driveway at Palisade. We had good occupancy. I saw a group of six or seven people gathered further down, waiting beside the kayak rack. Roxie must have a cave tour scheduled. The single yellow kayak that I'd bravely retrieved from the conniving Ned Nielsen in Grand Marais stood out from the others, which were blue and red, and I was encouraged by my contribution to the business. I slowed my pace to watch the Cook County man walk into the lawn, freshly cut by me, and point down at the ground twice before getting back into the truck and disappearing south on Highway 61.

SEVEN

On Saturday, fresh lumber was delivered ahead of schedule and off-loaded close to Number Eleven, just as I requested. The neat stack was imbued with its own special virtues, I adored the sweet smell of wood cured by the milling process. It was a timeless delight to my senses, and in a mystical way tied together the uneven stretches in my life. My starts and stops had been so frequent and varied that I needed a reminder from time to time that it was just one life and there would eventually be some sense made from my wanderings.

In the Northwoods, in my experience, something as routine as a lumber delivery was thought through and preplanned, and the material was always placed in the most logical location. In these parts there was no room for waste or wasted motion. Things had to be done once. Winter shapes your thinking and your process. The delivery crew no doubt looked over my project and put the wood where it made the most sense, as if they were fixing Number Eleven themselves. This was a silent covenant in the north—everyone gave a hand every day, in matters critical or minuscule. In the city, that stack of wood would have been dumped in the middle of the yard, with a few boards too twisted for carpentry.

It was sunny and calm and Superior looked inviting with an unwrinkled sheen. It was a perfect day to raise the wood frame, and I fetched a pair of sawhorses and ran power cords from the garage. I put a fresh blade on my Skil saw and knew that the boards would cut like butter because they were clear grained—a very satisfying experience for me. Roxie had left for Duluth the night before and said she would be gone for the weekend, if not longer. Ann was out at the picnic table sorting through the shards of the antique cuckoo clock that had belonged to her grandparents. She told me briefly that she had always wanted to live inside the clock when she was little, and her statement thoroughly perplexed me. I watched as she picked up each piece, turning it over and back again, rather helplessly. I decided to keep my distance for a little while, not wanting to seem intrusive, before I offered to help. I've repaired worse. The pieces were all there.

Roxie had evidently worked a deal with the lumber supplier in Hoyt Lakes and they tossed in four salvaged residential windows for free. They were all in good condition with workable sashes, but not uniform in size. I figured the smallest would work well for the bathroom, the two that matched would go in the kitchen, and the biggest one would be ideal for the new den facing the lake. I sketched out the framing plan from the sill plate up through the studs and headers to the roof trusses. I had to custom fabricate the roof to match the pitch of the remaining original roof. Ed Martini left behind dozens of pencil marks—dimensions, angles, and quick math—now left exposed by the damage. It gave me a very reliable map of the original structure. I didn't order much surplus lumber so I had no room for wasted cuts.

The original construction was expertly done, and I had the impression that the little house would stay standing even if you pulled out all of the nails. Its joints were meticulously fitted and tight as a drum. I envisioned a young Ed Martini standing in front of the newly constructed Number Eleven, donning a black-brimmed Amish hat, puffing on a corn cob pipe, and that humorous scene made me spit out my gum. I wondered how much Roxie looked like him. I predicted that Ann was the image of her mother, since there was nothing the least bit masculine about Ann.

By Sunday evening I finished the framing and hoped

to astonish Roxie with the swift progress. I saw an opportunity to add a small front deck on the lakeside, but I would need a power auger to put in three footings. It would have to wait, but I didn't want to forget my fine idea, so I added it to my drawing. A six-by-twelve deck would be perfect for Roxie and Caprice to watch the sunrise, which they did in lawn chairs in the wet grass already.

As I was putting away cords and tools in the garage, I was suddenly struck by all of it, that Palisade Point belonged to Ed Martini. His markings were everywhere. The simple precision of the installed shelving and the peg boards loaded with pliers and screwdrivers, all arranged around the singular principal of craft.

In the back of the garage, mostly covered by two sheets of plywood, I spotted the corner of a porcelain sign, a big one, maybe four by eight, the kind that the collectors pay big money to hang in their basement entertainment rooms. I had an affinity for these old signs. They were veritable works of art and have mostly disappeared from the American landscape, replaced by the garish LEDs and backlit plastic boxes that I detest. I dragged it outside with effort into the early evening pink light. The red, white, and blue were still brilliant and there was only a little rust starting along the bottom edge. It had a pearly white background with Titan Taconite Corporation in bold block letters. Underneath was the word Minnesota in smaller script. I leaned it up against the garage and planned to ask Ann about it in the morning.

Back inside, I was nearly finished when I looked up and saw sheets of paper tacked to the wall where the Titan sign had been stored. On closer inspection, it was bum wad—a thin, onion-skin paper architects used to sketch on when the world still valued hand-drawn ideas. There were two sheets of paper of identical size, one superimposed over the other, and together they depicted the layout of Palisade Point, with all eleven cabins and the long, looping gravel driveway. I flipped back and forth between the sheets and realized that the back sheet documented the original cabin configuration as purchased by Ed and Marie Martini. The front sheet showed the five additional cabins that Ed planned to build, and an expansion of Number One. He had creatively positioned the new cabins to even out the gaps and make the overall layout more efficient and pleasing to the eye. His initials, EMM, were in light pencil on the bottom right corner. I considered whether Ann and Roxie even knew this relic existed. It seemed like the sort of heirloom that should be curated like a museum piece and preserved. I mused that it was my first real exchange of ideas with Ed Martini, however silent the conversation.

EIGHT

The Morgenstern Golf and Country Club sat high above the winding northwestern bays of Lake Minnetonka, west of Minneapolis, like a crown jewel just beyond the reach of the masses. It was an architectural anomaly that intentionally copied some of the most notable buildings in Florence, Italy, specifically including elements from the Santa Maria Novella church, which was largely the model for the building's original design, as adapted for function as a country club. Later renovations modernized both the exterior and interior without diminishing the original vision, as so often happens with buildings over time. Morgenstern and its members were a sentient incarnation of the oldest money in Minnesota, stemming from the first ruthless European entrepreneurs who struck gold in lumber and iron ore, leaving permanent scars across the North Country. Membership in the club was by invitation and negotiated by patriarchs. The ranks did not noticeably vary year-to-year and bylaws were closely held. The first families of Morgenstern had remained largely intact over many years through genealogical scrutiny and informal alliance agreements. Commissioned paintings of club presidents hung in the prestigious Great Hall, whose walls were running out of room in Morgenstern's 150th year. That challenge would soon cause great consternation for those members aspiring toward portraiture. An earlier suggestion to relocate the oldest paintings to an adjoining room was met with a stern rebuke and one high-level firing.

In its early days, Morgenstern was a cool, fragrant, and secure oasis during humid summer days. An escape for the wealthy first families who lived in the limestone and granite castles in privileged neighborhoods across Minneapolis and St. Paul, places like Kenwood or Crocus Hill. Morgenstern was a brick-and-mortar covenant—a declaration of fresh nobility in the uncivilized and newly minted state of Minnesota. The sport of golf became an important focus later, in 1910, when Morgenstern acquired more land to extend the course to its present length. A renowned Scottish landscape architect named Edward MacBain was contracted for the redesign. He managed to include exact scale replicas of three holes from the Old Course at St. Andrews. This feature added further to Morgenstern's lore.

The chattering group gathered on a Saturday morning in the Great Hall. They were enjoying the conversations and somewhat reluctantly took their seats along two sides of the long marble table. The polished table was brilliant red with thin white streaks across the surface that resembled lightning frozen in time. The stone had been mined in the Languedoc region of France and imported for fabrication in Chicago shortly after the completion of the original Morgenstern. The atmosphere in the Great Hall was jocular, with much back-patting and handshaking. Early May delivered unimpeded sunshine that burst through tall stained-glass windows. The size and artistry of these windows would not be out of place in the great cathedrals of Notre Dame or Chartres, except for the images they portrayed. Hardly Christian, the windows depicted industrial construction: bridge erections, the setting of cornerstones, and armies of men in hard hats.

On cue, trays of coffee, tea, and Champagne were politely served by uniformed waiters. The chattering continued. A man entered the Great Hall and stood at the head of the table. He wore a natty, expertly tailored blue suit and soon gestured to someone hidden from view of the seated group. Then, stealthily, a massive electronic screen began a slow, whirring descent from its home high above the floor, in the thicket of exposed trusses that supported the vaulted roof. Once in position behind the man, the whirring noise stopped. The room was quiet. The black screen suddenly illuminated with video of a gentle mountain stream with sunny ripples. The words "Odin Forward" arose out of the moving water, coming into sharper focus as they grew bigger, much like the opening credits in a Hollywood movie.

The man smiled broadly. "Gentlemen, and ladies," he began, addressing a mostly male audience. He was fully energized, with raised eyebrows and then a humble bow that was not genuine. "I wish to welcome you all to the quarterly investors report for Odin Forward Properties LLC. Your patient and unflagging support for our organization has positioned Odin to finally achieve the spectacular returns we promised you in the very beginning of this endeavor. I believe you will be pleased with our stellar auditors report, our progress to goals, and our dependable projections for the next three years, and beyond."

There was spontaneous but modest applause by the group, many of whom exchanged thoughtful glances.

"Before we get into the numbers, by way of executive overview, I would like to share that the Blue Heron, our first investment, is beginning to exceed profit expectations despite its initial cost overruns. At the Heron, our only meaningful challenge now is capacity, and we are turning away customers for the first time. This circumstance, however unfortunate, is entirely solvable." The man in the blue suit was adept at detecting momentum shifts and he sensed the room was turning in his favor.

"For the love of God, Bill," said a voice from the rear of the room, "why do you need so many big words to say a simple thing. You dug yourself out and we're making money." Laughter and more applause.

Bill Trout did not appreciate any hint of disrespect. He had rather corvine facial features and a crow-like countenance. The applause subsided and Bill Trout continued. "My team has been relentlessly canvasing landowners between Two Harbors and Grand Marais for the past ten months. The master concept has always been to keep our Lake Superior resorts close enough together to share resources and amenities, but not so close that they start cannibalizing each other's profits. We can't afford to have them compete with each other. In another eighteen months, we will finish the construction of Sturgeon Shores, and it will be fully operational three months later. We also secured the last remaining land options to begin the initial permitting phase for Haven at Split Rock. When all three are operational, we will leverage one reservation system, one accounting department, one negotiated food and beverage contract, one rewards program, and we will control the three finest destination resorts on the north shore of Lake Superior. The economy of scale will be massive. There will be no other viable competition. Our guests won't be coming from Des Moines—they'll be coming from Malaysia."

The giant screen morphed again into a map of the North Shore showing color-coded parcels owned or controlled by Odin Forward. There were dozens of small dots scattered between the three Odin resorts. Bill Trout reminded that the smaller land holdings were strategic acquisitions intended to box out competition for many years. If Cook County ever sought eminent domain to open the way for competing projects, Odin could tie up the entitlement process with legal challenges, almost indefinitely.

Bill Trout pointed at the map. "Our data shows that a state-of-the-art fitness, spa, and sports facility in the right location would conveniently serve all three resorts. It is estimated that such a facility would instantly increase per key revenue by 15 percent. Again, data-driven, this will be a sixty thousand square foot facility with two gyms, cardio floor, interior lap pool, sauna, hot tubs, massage, salon, heathy eating café, and parking, with twenty-four/seven shuttle service from all three properties. A fifteen-minute trip at most. People will book our resorts and stay longer for this unique facility alone."

The group pondered this new development and small side conversations became scattered affirmative nods.

"The best part," Bill continued, "is that the new facility need not be lakeside. The right location, away from the shore, with the proper topography, will be far less expensive to acquire. It also comes with considerably more convenient trail connections to the Sawtooth Mountains. A win-win."

"We assume your team is all over that too," said the familiar voice in the rear of the room. "Not to interrupt, but several of us tee off in twenty-five minutes."

"Your Odin Forward team would never introduce an opportunity without a plan." Bill Trout winked his bird eye. "We need four to five acres, depending on shape. The most logical property is located right here." A rectangular shape on the map suddenly glowed bright green. "It's an obsolete resort called Palisade Point. The owner is dying. We understand it's seriously under water financially."

NINE

Roxie returned on Monday before lunch and I was struggling to remove the carburetor from the riding lawn mower. It was an older model John Deere, but Ed Martini had cleverly resuscitated it over and over with a variety of after-market and salvaged parts. The carburetor wasn't John Deere and was held in place by adjustable clamps. It was gummed up with old gas and oil. Caprice Wind bounced out of the passenger side of Roxie's VW and came straight over to give me an enthusiastic hug under Roxie's weather eye. She was a variation on Roxie, similar strong build and flowing black hair, muscular but still feminine. Her Chippewa facial features contrasted with Roxie's Martini side, particularly her flatter nose and rounder face. Other than that, it was not surprising that some mistook them for sisters. Ann had been right about that.

"Hello Owen! You were right Roxie, he's a handsome devil."

"I never said that." Roxie was incredulous, staring back at her disapprovingly.

"I've heard a lot about you too, Caprice," That was a stretch of the truth, but I was fairly entranced by the strength of her embrace and that our thighs made contact. I hadn't been touched like that by a woman in a while. She smelled faintly of wood smoke and even that it was attractive.

"You didn't hear anything about Owen from me," Roxie protested. "Jesus, Caprice."

Ann walked over from Number One. "Caprice, are you staying?"

"She might," Roxie interjected. "We're going to kayak the caves. It looks too smooth today so we might try it in the morning. The cabin looks good, Owen. Put the tarp back when you're done today. What's Dad's Titan sign doing outside the barn?"

"I just dragged it out to get a better look. It's a beautiful specimen and I've seen my share. Where'd it come from?" I asked, admiring the heavy metal rectangle leaning against the garage, even more colorful in daylight.

"Dad brought it home from the Mesabi when he took early retirement." Roxie squatted down to make a closer inspection of the sign's condition, frowning at some edge rust. "MHB used to be Titan years ago. It was the only thing he kept from his work life. Put it back where you found it Owen, before something happens to it."

"Mesabi comes from the Chippewa word for giant. Did you know that, Owen? Probably not." Caprice flashed a toothy smile.

"I did not," I said, while gently tugging the sign back into the garage.

Caprice confirmed she would stay the night and Ann offered to make Marie's signature lasagna, a family recipe going back three generations. The early evening was clear and cool but comfortable at the picnic table with a blazing cone of red oak in the fire pit. The meal was delicious and not at all like the lasagna I'd had in the past that relied on canned tomato paste and too much ricotta cheese. This lasagna was more about a combination of spices I couldn't pick apart, real tomatoes, finely grated cheeses, and firm wide noodles. Ann said she made the pasta from scratch, and I told her that I had never heard of such a thing. We passed around a bottle of merlot that a guest had left behind, still corked. Superior's lazy waves mellowed, suggesting a clear night was in the offing. Millions of faint light dots suddenly were visible overhead if you squinted. Roxie and Caprice reminded us again that they planned to set out in kayaks at daybreak if the water was rough enough.

"I rinsed off all of the life jackets and stacked them on

the workbench in the garage," I said, proud of my foresight and still uneasy about Roxie's ongoing evaluation of me.

"Good for you, Owen, but we don't wear them," Roxie responded, looking skyward at intensifying specks of light in the wide, open sky.

"You don't?" I asked, half seriously, thinking she was playing with me.

"Would you want to see a bullfighter wearing armor?" Caprice scolded me playfully.

"No."

"Of course not, Owen. Roxie and me don't just kayak. We challenge the big water, just like a couple of matadors in the ring. There's the difference. Anybody can kayak in calm water."

I finished my plate of lasagna quietly, listening to the three of them banter, cajole, and finish each other's sentences. It didn't matter that I knew I was their equal, that my own life's experiences put me on their level. I was rebuilding Number Eleven all by myself, from the ground up, using skills I'd honed ever since tinkering in my adoptive father's rented garage when I was twelve years old. But, facts aside, it was impossible to miss that they saw me as somehow subordinate, especially Roxie. I was the one grudgingly tolerated and expected to toe the line and follow the rules. For the time being, I didn't mind. They were wonderful creatures to observe.

"Caprice and I stopped to see Dad today," Roxie announced, looking over at Ann.

"How was he?" Ann answered defensively, staring at the pile of glowing coals, with their undulating white spots.

"He was peaceful, not agitated like last time. Probably the new meds are working."

"I need to go down and see him. Maybe I can just go with you next time? I don't think I can go in there by myself."

"That's a good idea." Roxie nodded encouragingly.

The sky gave in to the blackness of outer space, a magnificent canopy that can only be seen in the far north. A dome of stars enveloped us as the embers hissed and popped. There was no better place in the world than Lake Superior to appreciate the heavenly manifestation called the Milky Way, displayed in its entirety. There is a timeless quality to the night sky that made me feel alive and aware in two worlds: Earth and Heaven. It was simultaneously scintillating and unsettling. The thought that the Milky Way was always out there, suspended in space like a giant wheel, pulling us along for a celestial ride, but ignored or forgotten by most. Still, it was out there and always would be, while we are the definition of impermanence. I recalled a saying by a Sioux medicine man who claimed that the deadest you will ever be is while walking upon the Earth.

The wine was gone, but the female conversation went into overdrive, so I excused myself and got up to go to bed, yawning. Besides, the three women had abruptly moved the conversation from cooking to love making, which piqued my natural curiosity, but I expected uninhibited and embarrassing questions would come my way eventually. I had done enough for the day and was bone tired. In my new bed with the lights out, I could hear jazz music outside at the fire pit. And laughter. Bursts of shrieking girl laughter, lubricated with merlot. No doubt some of it was at my expense. I was quickly asleep.

TEN

After another week of sun and limited wind, I was ahead of my schedule for Roxie's cabin recon-struction. Number Eleven was fully enclosed and the windows were all installed, insulated, and working smoothly, earning a succinct compliment of "nice job" from Roxie Martini as she worked the sashes up and down. Roxie earlier had instructed me not to "fuck up the windows." I finished pulling the wiring, and the bathroom water connections were roughed in. I double-checked the placement of the pipes and was satisfied all were placed properly. You get that part wrong and the headaches are unending. Roxie's destroyed shower stall was a single and Ann said she complained about it whenever Caprice stayed over. It was quite simple to double the size since I was reframing the addition anyway, so I made an executive decision, again pondering my precarious relationship with Roxie. I needed to make a run to Hoyt Lakes for supplies, order the new fiberglass shower insert, and check on the timing of my drywall delivery. I thought momentarily about strapping a few sheets of drywall on the roof of the Camry, but my harrowing experience with the yellow kayak quickly chased away that awkward notion. I had another budding concern, too, about how well I could match the new and old shingles, get them close enough to pass muster with Roxie. Ordinarily I would have reroofed the whole structure, but I had an inkling she would be irritated by the waste of money to strip off and replace perfectly good shingles. Depending on continued good weather, I expected the cabin would be finished just ahead of Palisade Point's first sold-out weekend of the season, Memorial Day weekend.

Ann and Roxie left in the VW for Duluth to spend the afternoon with Ed Martini. Roxie decided to put off exploring caves with Caprice to another day, even though there were white caps starting to froth up on Superior. Caprice said it would do her good to nap in the hammock since she was a little hungover. She said she drank too much wine and red wine does that to her. I asked Ann if my snoring kept her awake but she said the wine nailed her, too. I found two empty wine bottles scorched in the fire pit, which was still smoldering with a thin smoke strand wafting upward.

My delayed drywall afforded me a half day off, so with the sisters Martini absent from Palisade Point, I set off on a hike up the Temperance River. I had a small, soft-sided cooler with a shoulder strap designed for hiking that I had almost forgotten about in the backseat of the Camry. I tossed in two beers and a cheese sandwich for the half-way point, wherever that might be.

The Temperance River State Park parking lot on Highway 61 was walkable from Palisade Point, so that seemed a perfect jumping-off point to wind upward to the highlands above Superior. There were only two cars in the lot, a Jeep and a Subaru, both new models and equipped with bike racks on the back ends. The nearly empty lot would be full by sunrise and the overgrown trails would be worn smooth by scores of stomping boots. After a quick check of my map, I decided it would be Carlton Peak first, then further on to Britton Peak. That would be a good first hike to build some much-needed stamina to take on the steeper inclines that lie beyond. Carpentry makes you strong as rope but does nothing for endurance.

The Temperance River is a churning, powerful wonder of nature. Deep brown from iron and spring-fed from the earth, it turns to a blizzard white as it explodes over a fifty-foot cliff and crashes down against deep basaltic canyons and stone gorges. Absorbing the phenomenon, I mused that it was the world's only five-story root beer float. Higher on the trail I could see a succession of three more falls, smaller in stature, one contributing to the next, with a collective roar that was intoxicating. The dense cover of pine, birch, tamarack, and oak protected the serpentine trail. I was fairly mesmerized by my surroundings and surprised I had stayed away from this region for so long. Too long. Erosion from the spring thaw produced a treacherous bend in the trail where much of it had fallen away down into the rushing frigid water below. I hugged the other side of the trail, putting one foot in front of the other, grabbing branches where I could.

Near Carlton Peak I came upon several craggy boulders that had split away from the rock formation and crashed down through the tangle until coming to rest in a heap. I had an unpleasant vision of Roxie at the sink brushing her teeth when the cabin was torn in two. The trail became a rock climb, and after another hour, I was at last perched on the summit. Superior glistened in the distance and the ferocious white caps rolled silently from my elevated vantage point. The Temperance River merely hummed now, sounding more like a yawning bear than a mighty river. The air was crisp, clear, and fragrant with thawing pine. I noticed an abandoned concrete foundation in the low scrub and recalled a note on my map that mentioned a fire tower that was removed from Carlton Peak in 1957. Almost due north and further inland, the stony outcropping of Britton Peak beckoned from high above the verdant carpet of treetops. It was higher than

Carlton, but the trail connecting the two peaks looked like a gradual rise and not overly challenging. I was encouraged by the break since my toes were cramping. Before setting off, I found a log bench and decided it was the perfect place to enjoy a beer and a sandwich. After all, this day was not one to be rushed.

I returned to Palisade Point hours later, in the late afternoon, to find the resort in the cloaking shadow of the namesake cliff to the west. An older gentleman was out walking the gravel driveway, slowly, with a cane in each hand. He shuffled his feet with some difficulty, taking determined, small steps. He wore blue jeans and a blue and black checkered shirt with the sleeves rolled up midforearm. Tufts of loose white hair peaked out underneath a straw fedora. His shoes had Velcro straps. Altogether he struck me as approachable, and I had an inkling it was Baskins, the author, who made annual treks to Palisade Point. I looped around to approach him from the front so I wouldn't cause alarm. He looked to be in his seventies, maybe eighties, but I was not good at guessing ages.

"Hello. Would you be Mr. Baskins?" I asked politely.

"I am," he answered with a generous smile and a wink.

"I'm Owen Martin. I'm working for the Martinis over the summer season."

"Good for you," Baskins said earnestly.

"If there's anything you need during your stay, just let us know and we'll get it taken care of. Maybe more firewood?"

"That's very gracious. Thank you, but I'm on my way in a few days and can't imagine a thing I need. Care to walk with me? I'm working my way around the circle, but I never know if I'm going to tip over, so the company would be appreciated."

"I'd be happy to walk with you. So, Roxie Martini said you're a writer?"

"I was. Not anymore. I used to think it was the Parkinson's that put an end to it, but I realized I had composed everything I ever set out to capture in words. Anything else would just dump it all back the grist mill and churn out the same ideas in a different order. That's a waste of time. Derivative. Now, I just watch birds, try to understand them. I think a lot about Jesus lately, too, for obvious reasons. I'm still trying to sort that out. It's interesting that God has you do all the important contemplation at the end of the line instead of the beginning. Seems backward to me, but it is what it is." Baskins's voice was gravelly, and he took short pauses mid-sentence to catch his breath.

"What did you used to write about?" I asked, hoping the question wasn't unwelcome because it sounded immature as soon as I said it.

Baskins stopped and closed his eyes briefly. "I always

admired the work of the great nature writers. People like Aldo Leopold, John Burroughs, Sig Olson—there are a few others, too, accomplished writers of that ilk, of that generation. I tried to emulate them, always prying open the connection between a man and the land he lived on. I have a theory that the land shapes you, and I am not being metaphorical here. I mean the place you choose to dwell alters you physically. In the modern parlance, I would say to you that nature has hold of your balls. It should come as no surprise to anyone."

"I'm not sure I follow."

"I wrote a story once for *Argosy* magazine called 'Many Lives.' The editor introduced is as a science fiction piece, which I found hilarious at the time because I knew precious little about science. The premise of the story was simple: If you had the wherewithal to create ten exact replicas of yourself, and you could place each one in a different location around the world to live out life simultaneously, say, one in New York City, another on Nebraska's rural plains, another on the island of Guam, another high up in the Himalayas, and maybe one right here on the edge of Lake Superior, you get the idea. Well, what I will tell you is at the end of their lives you would find ten very different people. They would still be you, but their voices would sound different, their relative health would be quite varied, their views of the world would be their own, and, most strangely of all, they would all look different, quite different, physically speaking. Therefore, I concluded, that one should be damn careful about where they spend their time."

"I think I would like an opportunity to read that story."

"Out of print for decades, unless there's an *Argosy* archive someplace. Only resides up here." Baskins tapped his temple.

"Where are you from, Mr. Baskins, if you don't mind me asking?"

"Originally the U.P. Later years, Taos, New Mexico. The weather there suits my afflictions. I fear this is my last time visiting Palisade Point. I have wonderful memories here."

ELEVEN

The silent ride became too painful to endure, so Ann finally interrupted the toxic quietude with a useless question as the VW flew by the dangling sign for Castle Danger. Roxie didn't respond and the car fell deathly quiet again. They'd been at Ed Martini's bedside for two and a half hours, waiting and watching for his eyes to open, hoping to see some confirmation of his awareness, that he would have the strength to acknowledge them, recognize them, if only for a second or two. Ed Martini's eyes never opened and it was Roxie who decided they had better leave and come back another day.

The nurse on call, who often covered the corridor that included Ed Martini's room, was a sad-looking, skinny fellow in blue-framed glasses named Marcus. He stopped by the room soon after Roxie and Ann arrived to explain patiently that Ed Martini's pain medication was increased again by hospice in recent days to assist his breathing. His waking moments were few now, and, if he awoke at all, it was for a few minutes first thing in the morning at shift change, when Ed's favorite came on duty. He knew her by voice but couldn't hold onto her name, it was so foreign-sounding to him. She was Nigerian. Ed used to motion for things he wanted with his unreliable but semi-functioning right arm, but Marcus said that the new meds seemed to shut that down. The daughters took turns holding Ed's right hand in theirs, a hand once so strong and thick, but now papery, bony, and cool to the touch. Roxie believed the bones might splinter if she squeezed too tightly, like holding a baby bird. Ed had made the choice to continue wearing his plain gold wedding ring after Marie passed. Sitting on the edge of the bed, Roxie stroked it gently with her pinky finger. She delicately turned it back and forth to check its security. It was so loose that it slid it off, making a pinging sound on the tile floor and rolled under the bed. Roxie quickly retrieved it and held it up for Ann to see before stuffing it into the pocket of her jeans. There were tears in both girls' eyes.

"Will you at least look at the offer?" Ann asked, looking the other way at the passing parade of rooftops in Castle Danger.

There was no response from Roxie, so finally Ann looked over at her sister.

"No need," Roxie said, "I'll never sign it." She accelerated to seventy knowing that the Highway Patrol favored this stretch of road.

Ann didn't realize she was biting her lip until the taste of blood registered. "Roxie, every single year we fall a little further behind. I haven't paid on our line of credit since last January and you know they watch those things. If the bank calls that line, we have no options. Palisade Point is the collateral for everything we owe. The whole thing is gradually eroding in front of us."

"I thought we broke even last year?"

"We worked like dogs last year. Those were your words."

"It wasn't perfect for Dad, either."

"The bank has the right to convert the line to a structured loan if we don't keep current. That means no more access to cash when we're short. You can't rent out a cabin without electricity. We have insurance premiums, and taxes. One unexpected problem would tip us over and now we have a way out. You pretend it all doesn't exist. I don't like it either."

Roxie pounded the steering wheel with a closed fist.

"If we lose Palisade Point to the bank, we have nothing. Then what? We start at zero somewhere else. I've never had another job and neither have you. I'm not ready for that. Are you?"

"If we are in such shit shape, why did you hire Owen? You told him he could stay through winter."

"We couldn't do it alone again this year. You don't realize, when you're gone kayaking all day, or in Duluth for the weekend, it's just me at Palisade Point. I get scared. I need help. Let's make what we can over the summer and sell out to Odin in the fall. One more summer dedicated to Mom and Dad's dream. Dad will never have to know. Owen will understand. He's not our responsibility."

"I'm not selling, especially not to those filthy bastards from Odin."

"You play with Caprice while I sit and stare at our books every day. It's not fair when we have the solution right in front of us, filthy bastards or not."

"You leave Caprice out of this. Dad would never forgive us for selling out. Don't you understand that? He wanted our family to own the resort for generations. That's all he talked about. Don't you remember?"

Ann exhaled slowly and paused, squinting out at Lake Superior's horizon, seeking to settle her churning stomach. "What are you planning to do with Dad's wedding ring?

"I don't know yet. I just didn't want them to lose it. It literally fell off his finger."

The racing VW went quiet again. Roxie pumped the gas angrily, then tapped the brakes, over and over, all the way back to Palisade Point. Losing her father forever suddenly became much more than a faraway abstraction.

Gray clouds gathered and easterly gusts buffeted the small car.

TWELVE

On Sunday morning at daybreak, I sat at the picnic table alone and sipped my steaming mug of coffee. Ann slept soundly and I appreciated the morning solitude. I glanced down toward Number Eleven, where I expected Roxie and Caprice to bound out any second in a flurry of female energy. As much as I delighted in my hike to Britton Peak, I was relieved to have a full load of drywall waiting for me in the garage: dry, carefully stacked and entirely undamaged, and delivered a little earlier than I expected. That was another thing I relished about working in the North Country. The full-timers, the year-rounders, the ones who lived in the north permanently, they were accustomed to unforgiving winters and seasonal bouts of poverty. To them, something as mundane as a schedule or a due date were for city dwellers, completely meaningless, serving no real purpose nor providing any added motivation. The only purpose or motivation was to help each other stay alive. I would get my drywall as soon as it was possible and practical, they said, whenever that is. But I knew that my materials were handled like pure and precious gold.

On cue, Roxie shot through the cabin door, banging the screen and dragging a backpack behind her. Then came Caprice toting a windbreaker. Roxie had on a yellow wetsuit that left no doubt she was an elite athlete. Caprice wore a similar wetsuit that was dark blue, nearly black, with white stripes up the sides. Caprice was a bit thicker through the hips than Roxie, but chiseled just the same. Seeing them from behind, striding together like a pair of Olympians, was impressive. Roxie and Caprice had long black braids that caught the early morning sun and glistened. Roxie backed up the VW to the garage and the two of them brought out the small trailer from behind the garage that was designed to carry two kayaks. I could have used that trailer on my Grand Marais pick up, but the Camry has no hitch. I wondered if Roxie knew that or just wanted to see how I would manage the rooftop contraption that nearly pulled my shoulder out of joint.

The two women loaded two blue kayaks effortlessly, as if the boats were virtually weightless, snapping each one into place with deft precision. They rumbled off down the road in their makeshift caravan. The lake was in a gentle roll, looking greenish close in, like a cloudy chunk of jade, and an eagle circled a mile above the Earth. I sat for a while, peacefully, feeling an abundance that was relaxing, sipping away at my steaming coffee. I stood to stretch and pondered the day's work sequence.

After coffee, I went inside the empty Number Eleven to staple additional insulation inside the exterior wall cavities, channeling my inner Ed Martini, the perfectionist craftsman. The staples were a proven method to prevent any sagging inside the walls due to gravity over time. By late morning, my stomach was in a low rumble, but I was excited to start the drywall installation. There was something so satisfying to me about working with drywall. The measuring, cutting, and snapping, the settings on my screw gun to perfectly bury the drywall screws without breaking the paper. Taping and mudding were even more glorious once you fell into the reliable rhythm. The smooth, semi-circular blading was a secret of the wrist primarily, and I proceeded inexorably around the room in a clockwise fashion. The task was, for me at least, a meditation or even a trance state. No thoughts intruded, just a smooth stroke at the perfect pace, much like the swing of a professional golfer, I was told once by one of the old guys. I never played golf. There was a framed picture at the Blue Heron of a golfer in knickers, standing on a green, holding up a silver trophy. It said his name was Bobby Jones.

Ann graciously brought down a tray around one

o'clock and I was famished, trance or no trance. She'd made a corned beef sandwich on rye that had my favorite Dijon mustard, with a dill pickle the size of a small salami, a molasses cookie, and a cold can of Fresca. It was better than any five-star restaurant in downtown Minneapolis. Ann traced the drywall seams with childlike wonder, leaning in to touch but stopping herself just short.

"Owen, I must say, you do good work. Is there anything you can't do around here? Frankly, not sure Roxie's worth it, but Dad would sing your praises if he was here. He was always frustrated by plastering. But his standards were too high I think. My Mom used to scold him for tearing things apart that he had just finished."

"I like his standards. You can tell he built this one right." I patted the wall. "Ed left me all sorts of hidden notes. Roxie wants it done for Memorial Day. I do work faster when she's not around watching, to be honest."

Ann stiffened. "Maybe, but when the families start rolling in for Memorial Day weekend, you won't still be working on this cabin. Right?"

"Don't worry. Roxie will have it all back before then, maybe just some painting and carpet left, but that can wait. So can the deck."

"Deck?'

"I decided to add a deck off the front, nothing fancy, just a dry platform for a couple of chaise lounges and a table for Roxie and Caprice to have coffee and watch the sunrise."

"Aren't you the romantic one," cooed Ann.

I felt my face flush. *What is it about these Martini girls?* "I'm just building up a little personal capital with your sister. We didn't get off to the best start."

"She agreed to pay for a new deck?"

"No, it's my treat. Really not much to it, a little lumber, a couple bags of ready mix, some hardware. It's low to the ground, no railing."

"Whatever you think best, and good luck with Roxie." Ann wrapped up the plate and utensils and carried the tray back to Number One.

Nearing five o'clock, I heard doors slam on the VW. The drywall was done and drying out with help from two purring box fans. The new kitchen, bath, and den took their shapes, looking far different from where I'd started ten hours earlier. I opened the windows to help clear out the humidity caused by the wet joint compound. I gathered up my tools and five-gallon pail and slipped away unseen as Roxie and Caprice tended to the kayaks.

THIRTEEN

The sea caves at Tettegouche were legendary. Roxie and Caprice put in at the mouth of Baptism River, about a half hour's drive south from Palisade Point. From there, they could explore Shovel Point and work down the coast to Palisade Head. Tettegouche State Park was a nine-thousand-acre reserve with two miles of rugged frontage on Lake Superior. Its high rock bluffs were honeycombed with sea caves that attracted recreational kayakers in calm conditions. When Superior turned angry, navigating the caves was dangerous, even for experienced kayakers. Outside of their group tours, Roxie and Caprice rarely explored the caves in calm water, preferring to work against the swells that made the interior passages into jagged gauntlets.

They reached Baptism River as a light rain began to fall and a layer of cottony fog hung above the roiling surf. Roxie gazed out along the horizon, scanning from north to south, assessing the conditions. If the weather remained relatively consistent for a few hours, she knew they would do all right. The trouble was, once they found the deeper caves, it was as black as a mineshaft and there was no way to gauge weather in the outside world. Roxie and Caprice believed that the darkest, most remote caverns belonged to them alone. The danger of the exploration fueled them both. Caprice trusted Roxie to command their treks together, which she did naturally.

Both women knew the network of caves by heart but also recognized that they behaved differently every day, depending on the wind, waves, temperature, and season. The caves were benevolent only in calm waters and only near Superior's coast. Inside the second cave, the light diminished to the point of shadows. Roxie guided Caprice with voice commands, sensing the location of the next opening, where total blackness reigned. They returned again and again to a hidden place that posed its own unique dangers.

A hundred yards inside the rock outcropping, Roxie stowed her paddle and relied on her hands to pull along the kayak in the still water. She closed her eyes at this point to aid her concentration. She gripped a familiar stone that signaled the place for a sharp left. Roxie twisted the kayak to align it with an even tighter passage through the cave wall. She felt around the opening with one hand. Caprice heard Roxie's kayak bump loudly against rock and it echoed. Roxie was certain that the water level would let them sneak through, but it would be a short visit since the lake was unpredictable and they could be trapped on the other side, if careless.

"First or second?" Roxie called out to her partner.

"I'll go," Caprice answered, moving her craft into position alongside Roxie. She slowed her breathing to relax her body, finding the mental rhythm that would carry her through to the other side. The size of the opening required Caprice to lie back against the hull of the kayak. She pulled herself through the short tunnel using familiar, but slippery rock formations as hand grips. One other time here, claustrophobia overcame Caprice and she abruptly tried to sit up inside the rock chute, suffering a badly bruised forehead that took weeks to heal. Roxie had to push her through from behind.

Caprice glided through without incident and the light on the other side hurt her eyes. She floated lazily, looking back for Roxie, who popped out of the black hole like a shiny cork. They both made it through. The two women grinned at each other in the burgeoning light, breathing deeply. They worshipped each other's courage, sharing the belief that very few people had the heart to explore, to put their lives entirely at risk. Roxie and Caprice sat floating in the twin kayaks, silently, in the voluminous subterranean pool, eerily lighted by dozens of twisted rock chimneys that connected the hidden chamber to the sky above. The only sounds were soft trickles of spring-fed water that danced down the rock walls. Roxie paddled to Caprice and they leaned together for an uninhibited, deep kiss, stroking each other's cold, wet hair. Roxie then paddled slowly to the center of the underground room and looked straight up into a speck of blue, glimpsing the outstretched wing of an eagle passing overhead.

"Roxie," Caprice said softly, her voice echoing subtly against the volcanic recesses. "I read a book once that said the Jewish people have an idea they call the Apocalypse. They say that's when heavenly secrets will explain human realities. It makes me think of this place. I think about why it's here. It doesn't seem like it's part of our world."

"What are you trying to say?"

Caprice paddled closer to Roxie. "I think your father is starting to leave the Earth. I feel him talking to the ancestors. That's how it starts when we leave the Earth."

The shafts of light intensified with an emerging sun. They floated together for a short time, listening to the falling water before Roxie decided it was best to leave.

FOURTEEN

From childhood, the Martini girls had a shared and palpable nostalgia for Memorial Day. Growing up at Palisade Point, Memorial Day weekend marked the end of their tedious bus rides to school down the coast in Silver Bay and heralded the tantalizing mysteries of a new resort season. They were tickled by the flood of new people and felt elevated because Ed and Marie Martini were the center of attention. The girls reveled in the instant camaraderie and good humor that permeated every square inch of the property as the first guests arrived in stuffed vehicles. It was the antithesis of desks and pencils and tiresome math lessons. On the weekend's first night, an array of circular fires glowed in front of each of the neat yellow cabins. The night air was no longer so cold, but refreshingly cool, seasoned by crackling hardwood. Ann and Roxie finally had their chance to play with dozens of boys and girls their own ages, making friends and alliances over the course of days that would stretch over years of return visits. The sadness of separation that ended each weekend was mercifully mollified by the next set of families soon on the way. In those early years, many of the same families returned season after season, with their own timeless memories of Palisade Point and a loyalty to Ed and Marie Martini, who were just like family.

When Roxie hit her teenage years, Marie's biggest concern shifted from finances to boys. She watched the youthful exuberance in the broad expanse, kids playing croquet, badminton, and horseshoes (in a pit Ed built) gradually give way to more furtive forays and walks in the woods that left Ann behind. There was no risk of embarrassment for Roxie, since the boys came and went so quickly. It was all so anonymous that there was little reluctance to push boundaries. Ed shrugged it off as natural teenage curiosity, which bothered Marie. Roxie was attractive at a young age and developed early, a siren call to boys sleeping a stone's throw from Roxie's bed. Roxie teased the boys until they asked for more. She called their bluff more than once and raised her shirt to reveal her bare breasts. She laughed at them when they retreated slack-jawed to their cabins with their hands in their pockets and their machismo damaged. Younger Ann never lifted her shirt for those boys but sometimes wanted to.

Ann busied herself with printed copies of emails at the kitchen table, checking arrival times, and verifying credit card deposits. A welcome early morning rain shower had softened the ground and made individual campfires far less of a worry, as it had been unseasonably dry. On Thursday, all but two cabins were full, and on Friday, Palisade Point would be sold out. Owen Martin had miraculously restored the riding lawn mower to a smooth-functioning condition and was circling the overgrown acreage with the blade set high, but still making a marked improvement to the lawn. He had found a box full of red, white, and blue bunting in a wooden crate in the garage labeled "July 4" and fixed them underneath the lakeside cabin windows, giving the buildings a festive and festooned appeal for the holiday weekend. Ann asked Owen to address the miserly amount of split birch and oak next to each cabin, although she conceded it was all neatly stacked to her satisfaction. Owen thought the firewood supply was more than adequate, but he agreed to add a couple of layers to each pile. Roxie's cabin, Number Eleven, was unfinished but entirely livable. Ann had gone to Two Harbors earlier to pick up ten boxes of Eskimo Pies that she peddled to guests at check-in. She anticipated plenty of questions about the menacing brown boulder in the front yard. She wasn't sure what to say, fearing that the truth would cause alarm.

A sleek black BMW turned into Palisade Point and stopped in front of Number One. Bill Trout slid out of the vehicle wearing his standard uniform, a finely tailored blue pinstripe with diamond-shaped sterling silver cufflinks that caught the sunshine. He was visibly annoyed by the gravel dust that began to descend on the pristine vehicle. He paced around the car like a frowning prison warden, dragging a finger across the finish.

"Mr. Trout?" Ann was peeking through a half-opened door. "I didn't expect to see you so soon."

"Greetings Ann, how are my two favorite Martinis? Still dry?" Trout said sardonically, still examining his BMW.

Ann grimaced. "Roxie hasn't even looked at it. We've been getting ready for Memorial Day." Ann was reinforced by the arrival of a silver minivan that carefully maneuvered around the BMW. It was full of young faces pressed against the glass. One little boy stuck his tongue out at Bill Trout.

"We're in seven," said the man in the driver's seat.

"Right over there." Ann pointed. "Get settled and stop back to register when you're ready. Welcome to Palisade Point." The minivan moved on to Number Seven and Ann looked back at Bill Trout, who shook his head at more dust sent aloft.

Bill bumptiously toed the grass with his black shoe. "No worries, Ann, I'm just here for meetings at the Blue Heron and checking on the construction of our new resort.

It's been a couple of weeks and I wanted to give our group some idea about your reaction, that's all. You do understand it's all cash?"

"No, I know that."

"That's pretty unusual."

"I can't speak for Roxie, but with the weekend, we'll be lucky to have time to shower, much less look at your letter."

"I understand. You have a business to run. How about next week?"

"We'll see." Ann looked over at Number Eleven and was relieved to see the cabin wasn't stirring. Bill Trout was the type of man that Roxie would engage for sport. Ann didn't need a surly confrontation with guests on the property.

Bill Trout turned to leave, then stopped short. "Ann, I have to ask, this land you have is worth a lot more than your family business. We aren't offering money for the buildings; they are incidental. We want the land. The buildings are worthless."

"To you, maybe, not to our family."

"Well, talk to any commercial land appraiser up here. Odin's offer is not just generous, it's twice what the place is worth. It's hard giving up the family business, but maybe you don't want to live your parent's life. If not now, when?" Bill was self-assured and satisfied with his final pitch. He had not rehearsed it. It came to him spontaneously.

"I'll keep it in mind."

"You know, Ann, doing our due diligence, we discovered that Cook County hasn't done a tax assessment review on this property in over twelve years. Way overdue in my opinion. We learned something else interesting, too. You ever hear of a county assessor named Gore?"

"No,"

"He and your dad were apparently quite friendly. Gore is retiring soon. Interesting when you think about it."

"I need you to leave now. We have people coming in all day today." Ann retreated behind the screen door, concerned that Bill Trout would notice the perspiration she felt on her brow. She had a momentary swirl of sour nausea in her middle.

Owen Martin came around Number Two riding the John Deere. He spotted the man in the suit and was suspicious and switched off the rumbling mower, keeping his eyes on Trout. Owen climbed off. As he approached the man, Bill Trout gave a quick nod in Ann's direction, jumped back into his dust-covered black BMW, and accelerated rapidly toward the Blue Heron. Ann looked over at Owen and wiped her hands on her blouse.

Just then, Roxie and Caprice staggered out of Number

Eleven in a laughing embrace, with arms and legs play-fully entangled, wrestling. They managed to separate long enough for Roxie to shout that she was bringing Caprice home to Duluth and that she'd be back by lunch.

FIFTEEN

I went through three tanks of gas mowing the grounds, going over the whole place twice to regain control over the scattered pockets of weeds and crab grass that grew faster and taller than the Kentucky Blue Grass that Ed Martini favored. I'd dug out and reseeded a couple of patches a week and my efforts were paying off. Next week I would be able to drop the blade one more notch, finally getting to the level that looked like a fine, green carpet. The John Deere spit out black smoke puffs for the first twenty minutes, then settled in and ran smoothly with excellent torque. I noticed the front right wheel wobbled slightly and would be sure to tighten the mounting nuts. Thinking about firewood, I pulled down a small chainsaw hanging from the garage rafters. It had an eighteen-inch blade, which was ideal, but it had a two-stroke motor and an empty gas tank, so I pawed around the garage to find any proper oil. I uncovered three plastic bottles of small engine oil stowed away in the bottom drawer of Ed's workbench. Fresh oil was preferred, but I knew this would work. Along the backside of the property there were scores of large limbs broken off by some past windstorm. I figured I'd use the chainsaw to get them apart in manageable sections, then cart some birch and oak branches back to the garage for splitting. I was ebullient. The prospect of labor more strenuous than the small muscle work rebuilding Roxie's cabin was invigorating. Carpentry and drywall involved more dexterity than force. I wiped down the chainsaw with a clean rag and inhaled the musty oil smell inside Ed Martini's garage. It transported me to the garage of my youth, perched on the edge of Miller's Lake, full of secret wonders for a young boy who spent hours twisting wire nuts and sorting screws.

Per Ann's request, the firewood was retrieved, sized, sorted, split and distributed to each cabin by lunch time, and she looked fairly in awe of my tenacity. It was a normal pace for me, and nicely soaked my shirt. I was accustomed to a contractor's cadence, abiding by well-established parameters for hourly production. If you fell behind on a task, the sequence was shot and it was a monumental task to get back on track. I mixed the birch and oak, since birch burns so fast, but people enjoy the sap crackles as much as the aroma of slow-burning oak.

There were new vehicles parked alongside Number

Seven, Number Three, and Number Eight, and I hoped they all caught sight of the neatly attended lawn. Young kids were outside of Number Three sitting at one of the picnic tables playing a game with a wooden box and dice. They were squealing and howling and nudging each other, finally freed from the stuffy confines of a backseat car ride. They all munched on Eskimo Pies in the sunshine with pieces of chocolate stuck to their lips.

The sun was higher in the sky by late May, and sixty degrees felt like seventy. Superior was kicking up furious white caps with green troughs. Incoming waves started their swell out to sea, gained height, then climaxed in an explosive curl, alive and majestic for seconds until mixing back into the big water. Ann filled a watering can from a hose connected to the backside of Number One. A ribbon of white and pink petunias, with tufts of purple meadow sage, encircled the cabin.

I caught her eye. "I think I'm all done with everything for the weekend, except for what's left to finish on Roxie's cabin. I'll wrap that up as soon as we empty out again. I'm headed down to the Heron to find a sandwich, if that's alright with you."

"Seriously, Owen, you don't have to ask. It's no problem. I know we need groceries, but I can't go to the market until Roxie gets back. I don't need anything else done for now. I can't quite believe you got the mower running like that." Ann stood back to check over her flowers.

A poster in the Blue Heron lobby promoted four consecutive nights of live music that would "convince you that Jimmy Buffett is in the room with your eyes closed." In the photo he looked Asian to me, but he had on the requisite Hawaiian shirt and sandals, so I deferred judgment, even though a Gordon Lightfoot impersonator would be far more appropriate on Superior's shore. Dean the bartender was holding court behind the bar at Keegan's, and the place was buzzing with new check-ins. He landed a punchline that I couldn't make sense of, but it instigated belly laughs and a couple of hand slaps on the bar. Dean saw me and worked his way over, grinning ear to ear.

"Owen, good to see you so soon. The Martini girls ready for the big weekend?"

"Yeah, we're in good shape. We're reserved out for Memorial Day."

"Us too. You should come over tonight to see Jonny Buffett. Bring the ladies. He was here last year. You won't believe how good he is. He's got live parrots on stage with him, too. How about a Balvenie for you?"

"Maybe a draft ale," I said happily, taking inventory of sore muscles asked to perform hard labor. "Something on the hoppy side. And a sandwich. You have a Reuben on the menu, Dean?"

"Yes and yes," Dean answered, eyeing more customers filtering in from the obstreperous lobby.

There was a low roar seeping into Keegan's as families shuffled from line to line to check in as quickly as possible and get their sixty-second orientation and a highlighted map to their accommodations. Dean said they would all be hopelessly lost without an illustrated route to one of the grand suites on the top floor or to one of the surfside condos down the coast. People trudged away pulling along wheeled suitcases, engrossed in their maps and looking around for signs. Dean said that by tomorrow they would know the place by heart.

I thought about Ann and Roxie, and poor Ed Martini languishing in a nursing home down in Duluth. *What would Ed make of the Blue Heron?* It probably would make his blood run cold or reduce him to tears, knowing what he was up against. I learned a long time ago to never punch above my weight class. I tried that once and woke up in an emergency room. I could see now that Palisade Point didn't have a puncher's chance against this money machine.

Dean brought over my beer and Reuben. He was in his element and seemed to bask in the glow of a bar full of new friends with fat wallets.

"Enjoy!" Dean gave me an exaggerated hand flourish as he deftly slid the loaded plate across the bar.

"I didn't realize how famished I was until I sat my ass down." It was the truth.

"Owen, tell me, where are you from, originally?"

"Originally? I couldn't say, moved a lot, but I remember the years living on a little lake in southern Minnesota. Miller's Lake." I pictured my adoptive father, Sam Martin, who remained youthful and handsome in my memories. For many years I had made sporadic and clumsy attempts to locate my birth parents with no solid leads—but a handful of confirmed dead ends. I would find myself looking for my features in the faces at a hardware store. Ridiculous. The disappointments were harder and harder to shake and my only effective salve for the sting of the orphan was physical labor. I eventually stopped trying, but the idea occasionally resurfaced to club me over the head.

"From a little lake in southern Minnesota to the biggest lake in North America. It must be in your blood." Dean said, leaning left to peel a credit card off the bar with fat fingers.

"That might be true," I said.

At night we were all exhausted. We knew the cabins would be filled soon and Ann said there would be a litany of special requests and maybe a complaint or two, so be prepared. The weather began to cooperate, although the warmer days still succumbed to darkness in the upper forties. I sat around the fire awhile with Roxie and Ann, who were both contented and quiet. I'm sure they were pondering the past and thinking about how much their dad would admire the clear starry sky while tuckered children slid into warm beds inside his cabins. Marie Martini would be at his side, holding hands. It seemed to me that Ann and Roxie Martini were bound to this land by nurturing familial tentacles wrapped snuggly around their ankles.

"I'm going to bed," Roxie whispered with eyes closed, and she stood to stretch before ambling away toward Number Eleven, illuminated by the moon and stars.

"Good night, Sis, see you in the morning," Ann muttered, mustering her remaining energy.

A light in the kitchen flicked on and a silhouette of Roxie appeared and it looked like she poured herself a drink. Then the window went black.

"Me, too, I guess," Ann said to me, sleepily.

"Take your time," I said. "I'll give you a head start on the bathroom. I want to let the fire die down a little more before I come in. I'll shovel a little dirt on top."

Ann crept languidly toward Number One, her arms at her side, looking childlike with a fleece blanket draped over her shoulders. Mighty Lake Superior growled in the distance, reveling in the night. Even though civilization had taken root along the North Shore over past decades, the big lake remained as brutal and patient as ever. It had nothing to fear from us.

Later, I was pawing around a kitchen cupboard for a shot glass when I found a faded Polaroid taped to the inside of the door. It was a picture of Ed and Marie Martini leaning against either side of the Palisade Point sign. It appeared newly installed (there was a shovel on the ground) and the owners were beaming. Ed looked young and strong with short black hair, combed back, and crisp tan slacks with a thin black belt. Young Marie was basically Ann, no question, the smile and tilted head were unmistakable.

I brushed my teeth and decided to quickly shower since my dried sweat had turned disagreeable and I always slept better clean. I relished the silkiness of cool, clean sheets and opened my window an inch to fill the room with fragrant night air without making the cabin cold for Ann. I was on the verge of sleep when I realized Ann had slipped under the covers and nestled her slight frame against mine. She didn't make a sound and I didn't dare to either. I was awake again. Her warm body fit perfectly against the cruder contours of my own and her light snoring was trust incarnate.

SIXTEEN

Memorial Day weekend was uneventful in the sense that there were no catastrophes beyond a simple plugged toilet that I remedied with a plunger and sheer muscle. The power stayed on (a concern in the past according to Ann) and no one got hurt hiking or climbing, always a risk when city dwellers take to trails without preparation. The mothers and fathers stayed relatively sober, and there were still high hopes, Ann said, that none of the checks would bounce. In short, she said it was their best opening weekend since taking over the operation after Ed Martini's untimely stroke. Ann was energized and restored, almost feline in her quick and assured movements. I allowed myself to dream that her night in my bed could have been the real source of her bliss, but the thought was hard to hold onto. I questioned whether it really had happened or was instead all in my mind. My bed was, after all, empty when I woke and not a shred of evidence was to be found. I looked.

By Wednesday morning, I was well into my new routines and getting ready for the next assemblage of guests who would start arriving on Thursday. The grounds were already a little shaggy, so I was back at the gas tank drawing off five gallons at a time for the John Deere. I asked Ann over scrambled eggs and smoked bacon when we might see Caprice again. She said Caprice showed up less often in the summer because she didn't like to be around so many White people, for religious reasons. Roxie told Ann it was unwise to poke around too much in Caprice's thinking—that it might be disturbing.

"Can you drive us down to Two Harbors for groceries today? I need to make a deposit at the bank too," Ann asked with an inviting smile while delicious smoked bacon grease hung in the air.

"If we go now, all the better, I can mow right after lunch." I liked the idea of a car ride to Two Harbors with Ann next to me.

"Roxie is around this morning. It's just the writer here and he never asks for anything. Remind me to buy Eskimo Pies. We're almost out," Ann said, scanning her list.

We got in the Camry after I cleaned out the accumulated paper cups and wrappers strewn across the passenger side and headed south on North Shore Drive. Traffic was heavy, so I could only catch a quick glimpse of the mustard-colored Split Rock Lighthouse and later the dense pine forests at Gooseberry Falls. We sailed through a modern miracle called Silver Creek Cliff Tunnel, a passageway blasted through a stone mountain. The mountain tunnel was artificially lighted, neatly tiled, and well over a thousand feet in length. Prior to the construction of the Silver Creek Cliff Tunnel, the old North Shore Drive wound its way precipitously around the mountain with little to protect vehicles from a fatal plunge into the lowlands below. Further south a similar but shorter tunnel called Lafayette Bluff delivered us to the outskirts of Two Harbors.

The terrain flattens when you descend into Two Harbors, and a heavy industrial apparatus takes over the landscape. The menacing steel and concrete structures were designed for the sole purpose of conveying hundreds of thousands of tons of iron ore to docked ore ships. We stopped for coffee at a small café that had an unpretentious wine bar inside and an ice cream freezer with a service window to a patio outside where people walked up for cones and sundaes. It was already bustling, but we found two open stools at the counter. I ordered a large black French roast and Ann asked for something called a white mocha latte with almond milk, whipped cream, and dark chocolate shavings. It smelled wonderful but was not the caffeine jolt I was after.

When we pulled into the grocery store parking lot, I

noticed the cart corral was full and I thought it best to grab one in case they were all outside. Ann squeezed my arm and appeared to have an epiphany.

"What?" I asked, thinking I had found the wrong grocery store.

"Let's keep going. Groceries can wait. Let's go to Duluth and see my dad. I want you to meet him. We're almost there anyway. I need to see him today. Okay?" Ann pleaded softly.

I was confused by her sudden change in tone, from silly to serious, but I didn't see any reason to object, as long as I had enough daylight hours to finish my work.

"We can go on to Duluth, no problem." I said, instantly concerned that Roxie might feel threatened by my meeting their precious dying father. This was their private affair, not mine.

"It can be a quick visit. He'll be asleep anyway."

Off we went another half hour to Duluth. Ed's facility was up the bluff from the downtown, itself built into the hillside with views of the harbor and the historic Duluth lift bridge. Duluth's streets were steep and crowded. Winter's ice made them downright harrowing to navigate, and I was grateful to see them bone dry. We found the place called Hearthstone Skilled Care. It was managed by a group of Catholic sisters that I had never heard of. Something about Saint Vincent. Hearthstone was a single-story building with two wings veering off a central core. It was older but dutifully maintained and freshly painted bright white. Some of the windows had lost seal and were cloudy and I thought that was very sad for those trapped inside. The young Latina receptionist in the lobby recognized Ann and briskly waved us through with a warm smile. Ann said her name was Aurora and she was a nursing student at the University of Minnesota in Duluth.

I trailed Ann down the long, polished corridor with two shiny wooden railings firmly attached to the walls. There was a desiccated, ashen man in a wheelchair, motionless, watching Ann with milky eyes. He was held in place by a wide red strap around his belly. We passed by and he struggled to turn his chair. Further down the hall, a whiff of bowel emanated from an open door that made me cover my nose out of instinct. Near the end of the corridor on the right side was Room 115. Ed Martini was inside, sound asleep in a hulking mechanical hospital bed, with the back raised thirty degrees. In his waking moments, it looked like Ed was positioned to gaze out the window toward the Port of Duluth and the lift bridge. I was relieved to see his clear window. Ann said she and Roxie paid extra to get the room, knowing that the view would soothe his anxieties.

Ed Martini was sleeping peacefully.

"Hi Dad," Ann whispered in his ear and took his

twisted hand in hers. "Dad, I brought a friend today. His name is Owen Martin, and he's helping us with Palisade this summer. He's a builder like you are. Everything looks so good this year. Just the way you like it." Ann's voice broke.

Ed opened his eyes, one noticeably wider than the other, and Ann leaned in closer with anticipation. Ed blinked with recognition.

"Hello Mr. Martini," I said, woefully unsure of proper etiquette in the situation, feeling the floor turn to sand. I had no direct experience with the end of life, and I stood there exposed in its ebbing presence. I had only heard of such experiences second hand, after the fact, and it was harmless at a distance, like when I was told as a boy that the coin collector John Chambers shot himself a week after it happened. It wasn't real. Ed Martini was reed thin under a mint green blanket. His long arms were once muscled and strong, I knew, but not anymore. Someone shaved his face and combed his hair with a straight part on the left side. There was a framed photo of Ed, Marie, and young Roxie and Ann on the bedside bureau. Roxie was holding an orange cat.

"Dad, I wanted you to know that we had a sold-out Memorial Day weekend. All of your cabins were full up, and we are starting off the season flush with cash, but don't worry, we'll be careful just like you always were.

Owen got the mower going and the garage is organized again. We had lots of kids running around everywhere. Next weekend looks just as good. Dad, can you hear me? How are you feeling?" Ann was speaking nervously, aware that Ed's attention was usually fleeting.

Ed raised his opposite hand and gave us a rudimentary thumbs up, but his digits were clenched and uncooperative. Ann started to cry and retreated into the hallway. Ed motioned me closer and tapped his tangle of fingers on my chest twice.

I felt obligated to take over for Ann, who I could hear sniffling outside the door. "Mr. Martini, I put a new carburetor on your John Deere and it turned right over. Nothing wrong with that mower. I sharpened the blades and made quick work of your big lawn at the Palisade."

Ed Martini pursed his lips and gave me a knowing nod. He closed his eyes and dropped back into his slumber. I looked over what remained of the man and felt the sudden weight of his many ambitions and the love he held for his family, for his land.

SEVENTEEN

Bill Trout was visibly exasperated by the grindingly slow numbers rotating on the gas pump. The pump was one of two, and both looked frail, listing toward the lake on a sinking concrete pad. A light rain had begun to fall and dark spots were collecting on his slate gray wool suit. Bill Trout detested the smell of wet wool. He wiped his face with a red silk handkerchief. Finally, the tank topped off and he proceeded toward the store, the only gas and grocery in Schroeder, Minnesota.

The man behind the register gave him a nod.

"I ask you," Bill Trout said as he approached the man. "Why am I forced to use a goddamned gas pump from the nineteen fifties, answer me that?"

The manager looked out the window at the car, amused, noting in particular the sticky red clay stuck to the fenders of the man's black BMW. He turned back around to Bill Trout. "My brother-in-law owns a car wash down in Silver Bay. I've got dollar-off coupons if you want one. It's called the Suds Zone. You go right by on sixty-one."

"No thanks."

"We sell umbrellas, too."

"You're a funny guy. Just the gas." Bill Trout aggressively patted his pockets until he found his wallet. He peered up at the sky. "Is it supposed to rain all day?"

"On and off," answered the manager, who was now busy sorting packs of cigarettes on the counter.

"Really, what's the deal out there? It took forever to fill up. Are you bone dry?"

"You answered your own question pal," the manager calmly replied, stacking up Kents, Pall Malls, and Lucky Strikes.

"What?"

"It's a pump. You said it. It pulls gas out of the underground tank. It's slow by design. The new stations, the one's you're probably familiar with, they don't have pumps at all. They have electronic gauges that just look like pumps. The underground tanks are pressurized to shoot the gas up through the hose at lightning speed. That's not a pump. Completely different technology. You must not know that." The manager loaded the overhead dispenser with cigarettes, gently tapping the packs into place.

Bill Trout stared at the man, shaking his head. "My

suit's wet. That's what I know."

"You smell a little like wet dog."

Bill Trout drove south from Schroeder about three miles on North Shore Drive until he spotted the low-slung silt fencing surrounding the property that would become Sturgeon Shores. The investors were on the way for a ceremonial groundbreaking over the weekend. Bill hoped that enough rough grading had been accomplished to provide a clean and level space to park and set up for the event. Rain wouldn't help. The design team for Sturgeon Shores was landing in Minneapolis on Friday night and he was counting on them to remove any lingering doubts about a resort even bolder than the Blue Heron. Bill Trout was shifting the calculus for North Shore hospitality. That was the plan.

The architect's charge was to create such an unprecedented design that existing zoning codes would be neutered, incoherent, leaving room for new, more convenient standards that were loose enough to allow large structures at the water's edge. An organic fusion of luxury and nature is what they called it. That's what Bill Trout had promised in the beginning at the first investors' meeting at the Morgenstern Golf and Country Club.

Trout was edgy and apprehensive when he pulled onto the shoulder. Two enormous yellow graders were scraping damp earth, smoothing the natural terrain for excavation. The churning of the heavy diesel provided Trout with some relief, but he understood that Sturgeon Shores was a far bigger gamble than the Blue Heron—much more complex financially, with a web of commitments and assumptions that he alone fully comprehended. The investors were told as little as possible about the structure of the deal, the financial clockwork that Trout tinkered with every waking hour. He could not afford to lose the confidence of even one investor. Any misstep would roil the deal. The Blue Heron had been their beachhead. Sturgeon Shores would launch Odin Forward Properties to the stratosphere. It would jump-start Haven at Split Rock, in Lutsen—another similarly complicated deal with a thousand moving parts. The ultimate master plan relied on all three properties operating simultaneously and at full bore. Anything short of that and the house of cards would come down. Bill Trout had many promises to keep.

Bill Trout watched the activities from his car. The light rain was subsiding as the graders finished leveling a large pile of gravel near the entrance to the site. A crew of carpenters had arrived on time to assemble a wooden dais that would hold the visiting dignitaries and designated speakers for the event. A white vinyl tent was on order and would be erected to provide protection for the dais. That crew dragged out rolls of green outdoor carpeting from one of their vans. Bill Trout checked his watch and glanced up and down North Shore Drive. The design team promised mounted renderings of Sturgeon Shores that would nicely frame the stage, illustrating myriad unique features, including a next-generation microbrewery contained inside a thirty-foot tall glass box. Bill Trout had arranged for three security guards from the Blue Heron to direct vehicle parking and to shoo away any curious interlopers.

Despite the progress of the workmen, he had serious reservations about the event itself. Only one of the investors was willing to say a few words. The group preferred, by nature, anonymity. But they all, somewhat grudgingly, agreed to stand together for a groundbreaking photo with golden shovels in hand. Minnesota's governor committed to attend and proclaim his support for Sturgeon Shores, giving the event the sheen of high office. A conflict at the Capitol made him a late scratch, and that worried Trout. The mayor of Schroeder generously offered to stand in for the governor, and Trout felt obligated to accede, reluctantly. Mayor Vernon Tung was no Governor of Minnesota. He was inarticulate and poorly dressed, with an affinity for plaid jackets. Trout would have to count on his Chicago architects to be the centerpiece of the program. Mayor Tung's spotlight moment had to be diplomatically controlled, a few words, simple and reassuring. The event had to deliver unencumbered awe, unbridled enthusiasm, and ample congratulatory applause. If the Minneapolis media didn't disappoint, the public relations bonanza would prove invaluable. A gust of wind picked up a cloud of fine sand and peppered Trout's black BMW. Annoyed, he checked his watch.

EIGHTEEN

Roxie said she was leaving early for Duluth, so it made sense to lay the carpet and set the bathroom tile in Number Eleven before another busy weekend swallowed me whole. I set my alarm for five and was up in time to admire the glow peeking above the horizon line that bathed the big water in undulated streaks of blue and orange. It had been a few years since I'd set tile, and I rehearsed in my head how you sponge against the seams, always against, otherwise the grout comes right back out again. I enjoyed grouting almost as much as working with drywall and looked forward to the trowel and wet sponge. I thought about squeezing in a break between tile and carpet to run up to Grand Marais to visit a used bookstore I saw when I picked up the kayak from Ned the outfitter. I gave up trying to read my book on medieval armor. Maybe it was too foreign a subject to contemplate in the presence of Lake Superior. I couldn't get past the first few pages. I figured I might trade it if the shop takes trades.

Maybe a book on Superior shipwrecks, birds, or Indians.

I made a second cup of instant coffee in a crockery mug that had a handle in the shape of an antler. Ann said that mug was her dad's favorite so to be careful. She was sound asleep when I slipped out the front door to the picnic table. The sun had broken the horizon line, and the eastern sky was alive with gauzy purple and blue shapes that resembled a collection of frosted cakes floating in air. The only sounds were a few squirrels scratching their way up and down the pines in utter delight. I could see their quick bushy tails darting between the branches.

I heard the screen door shut on Number Eleven and looked up to see a man walking away from the cabin with his head down and his hands in pockets. The oddity of the scene stunned me. I watched him reach the road's shoulder, where he turned and proceeded down the road. For no good reason, I put down my coffee and started jogging after him. I got closer and saw he was uniformed, looked like the man from Cook County who was talking out front to Roxie weeks ago. He heard me approaching and started running. There was a pickup truck parked alone in the public lot at Temperance River. It was a county truck. I picked up the pace and was gaining on him.

I grabbed the back of his shirt and spun him around. He was out of breath and about my size but paunchy with a puffy face. "What were you doing at that cabin? Who are you?"

The man threw a haymaker at my head, but I ducked and it missed me completely. Instinctively, I returned a right hook, a hard one, that connected right below his nose. I had been in enough bare-knuckled tussles over the years to know the sound of a broken nose. The bones gave way with a wet click and he dropped to his knees instantly, cradling his nose with both hands, blood streaming out between his fingers. The blood looked black in the dim light.

"You broke my nose!" he screamed at me with squinted eyes. "You didn't have to break my nose. Damn it!" He tried to stand but went back down to one knee.

"Tell me what you were doing in that cabin!" I was bursting with adrenaline and looked around quickly, relieved to see no vehicles coming from either direction. I was probably in trouble again and already regretted the punch.

I heard Roxie bolt out of Number Eleven. "Leave him alone, Owen," she shouted at me sternly and went back inside with a door slam.

"Get going." I said to the man, who was dabbing his face with his sleeve. The snapped bone in his nose had opened a gash across the knuckles of my right hand. I was dripping blood too.

The uniformed man stood with difficulty and was

wobbly, still covering his face with one hand. The front of his shirt was soaked. "I'm red tagging you, son of a bitch!" He staggered toward his truck, stopping every few steps to check on me. I watched him start the truck and drive out of the Temperance River parking lot.

I struck him too hard, I concluded, or, at least harder than was necessary. He wasn't much of a challenge, *but how could you know*? I was not exactly a bruiser by any measure, but years in the trades gives a man strength that belies appearance. I needed to check on Roxie, but the situation left me flummoxed and therefore apprehensive. Ann was scurrying down the hillside in her bathrobe. I waited to follow her inside.

"Roxie what's going on?" Ann was raspy and her slippers were wet from dew with grass clippings clinging to them.

"Some guy was trying to pry open my door," Roxie dismissively explained while staring straight at me.

"I went outside with my coffee. He saw me and started running. Must've scared him off." It was essentially the truth. I picked my words carefully, not knowing where Roxie's story was headed.

"God Roxie, that's terrifying. We have to call the police."

"No Ann, we don't need the police here. It was no big thing. He was probably drunk in his truck. He won't be back. He knows we have Owen here. Owen let him have it."

Ann examined the door. "Looks okay. He didn't do anything to it."

"I scared him off before he had much of a chance to try that door. It was locked, right Roxie?" I felt the need to elaborate, but immediately wished I had kept my mouth shut. My injured right hand started screaming at me.

"Always locked at night."

Ann was shaken, but composed herself with a few deep breaths. She offered to make us all breakfast, shaking her head in disbelief, shivering in her apricot robe and wet slippers. Roxie eyed me, tight-lipped, and made it clear that there would be no further discussion of the incident. Roxie told Ann that she was going to Duluth after breakfast to spend the day with Caprice. A strange start to everyone's day, to say the least, but I would be able to tackle the carpet and tile as planned. I retrieved my antler-handled coffee mug and offered to help in the kitchen.

"With that hand?" Ann asked.

I looked it over. The bleeding had stopped but it needed attention and my knuckles started turning purple. My fingers moved with difficulty. This one would take a while to heal, but I figured I could work with it. Ann made me soak my hand in a mixing bowl full of peroxide, which felt like an acetylene torch. She dried it off and applied antiseptic ointment from a tube and two butterfly bandages. She poured me a short glass of Jameson that I normally wouldn't drink in the morning, but it helped with the pain.

NINETEEN

By the middle of June, the money side of Palisade Point must have improved, since Ann and Roxie weren't arguing as much about expenses. Roxie's kayak excursions were running at capacity, and she was turning people away, with only a date or two in August still open. Ann admitted the kayaking proceeds bolstered the bottom line more than she could have imagined when Roxie came up with the idea. She originally believed the cave tour plan was a ruse to justify new equipment for her and Caprice. It may have been true, but I guessed it didn't matter anymore. Dean, the bartender at the Blue Heron, told me people were talking about Roxie at the bar, raving about her expertise in the sea caves at Tettegouche. She was gaining a reputation as a sought-after guide, which didn't surprise me.

The end of June delivered an unwelcome poke in the eye with a last-minute cancellation that proved impossible to refill. The Magnusson family was second generation, very loyal to Palisade Point, so Ann felt compelled to refund their deposit, which she would have kept under normal circumstances, and it left a stinging hole in June's revenue. What made it doubly painful was Ann's discovery that the family moved their reservation to the Blue Heron, where they were on a waiting list. The Blue Heron was hosting a hot air balloon festival, with free rides for guests on Saturday and Sunday. Mrs. Magnusson explained they simply couldn't pass up the opportunity to take their kids on a balloon ride above Lake Superior. She apologized to Ann for the short notice and assured her that they'd be back at Palisade next year. It tossed Ann into a quiet depression.

Number Three, Seven, and Eight would stand empty and lifeless on one of the best weekends of the season, weather-wise. The peak temperature was seventy-four, with a cloudless sky, low humidity, a gentle breeze from the south, and smooth water. This was more the way Superior behaved in Bayfield, Wisconsin, buffered and protected by the Apostle Islands. The unwelcome cancellation was beneficial in one respect, at least for me, since we had toilet problems again in Four and Five that needed immediate attention. Ann moved the guests into Seven and Eight, and I snaked the commodes for hours without much improvement. The toilets stubbornly refused to flush properly, with a weak siphoning effect. Grayish water percolated up through the shower drains, and that was a distressing development. I suspected tree roots infiltrated the main drain line to the septic tank—I had seen that happen before with similar symptoms. There was no way to know for sure without sending a camera through the line, and that costs big money. I rented a longer sewer snake in Silver Bay, a thirty-footer, to try and bust through the obstruction. It helped a little. I worked the new snake for another hour until my shoulders burned. I strongly suggested to Ann that we bring in a real plumber for the job, but she resisted, insisting that the problem was probably temporary and would resolve itself. The cabins were vacant for the weekend anyway, she said, so we should just give it rest. I said that a "rest" was highly unlikely to accomplish anything, but we could give it a try.

After the toilet debacle, I mowed the grounds. It was restorative for me when I finished the task far quicker than my first effort back in April. I had the course down pat and ran the John Deere in high gear the whole way. I washed up before meandering down to the Blue Heron to watch the balloon convention. The parking lot was full, so the Blue Heron was at maximum capacity. The Magnussons were lucky to get in. Cars full of gawkers were pulled off along both sides of Highway 61, with windows down and heads peeking out. I counted nine balloons already aloft, floating inland to the northwest, like a collection of giant striped Easter eggs against a blue topaz sky. A tenth balloon, bright red, was tethered in the grass with its passenger basket secured to steel stakes by thick straps. A technician in a white jumpsuit was frantically giving animated instructions to the next group of riders, who weren't paying much attention. There were cameras out everywhere. The group of a dozen or so were escorted to the basket and helped aboard. A young boy burst into tears, bawling, and he refused to get in the basket. A stiff jerk on the arm by his mother settled him down. A brass quartet in laughably exaggerated military uniforms was situated at the base of the towering Blue Heron pylon sign: bright red and white jackets with silvery tasseled epaulets the size of mopheads, and vertical rows of big brass buttons. They struck up a Dixieland melody with two trombones honking away. The pilot in the basket pulled an overhead lever, igniting a hissing torch that turned the balloon's belly into a blast furnace. The straps were loosened, and the balloon and basket lifted gracefully up into the clear late afternoon sky. The gathered crowd applauded and whistled wildly with the quartet at full throat. A snare drum joined in. It was an impressive sight.

I walked to Palisade Point, glancing back over my shoulder occasionally at the inspiring array of balloons.

Ann was out front at the picnic table smoking a long filtered cigarette. She held it like a rookie between her thumb and forefinger.

"I've never seen you smoke before."

"I don't, but sometimes I do. Owen, you've got me worried about the plumbing problem. If we can't keep these cabins filled, all of them, we won't make it through the season. I have taxes due in November. The season's half over and we're not at break-even yet. And that's assuming my tax bill doesn't have a surprise for me."

Ann took a deep draw off her cigarette and coughed. I had never worried much about money. When I ran out, I found work and got paid in cash, sometimes the same day. I didn't owe anybody anything. Here was Ann, clearly trapped by the obligations she inherited, looking at me forlorn, imploring me for solace, maybe pretending for a moment that I was her cherished dad, Ed Martini.

"I think we were doing pretty well," I said, knowing nothing of the place's finances.

"Cash comes in alright, but it burns quicker than you can imagine. Gas and electric jumped this spring. More than that, Dad's bills keep coming from Hearthstone. Every new medication is more expensive. Roxie could charge more for her sea cave tours, too, but she won't do it. I don't understand why."

"Ann, just stop paying me for a while, at least until we

get the plumbing figured out. I have everything I need. Maybe use that money to get an actual plumber out here to look it over."

"That's not fair to you."

"Think about it, Ann. I've got enough saved up to carry me, and it costs me next to nothing to live here. I'm fine."

"It's just not fair. Dad wouldn't do that."

"I'm saying it's an option. Only short term. I don't mind at all. Roxie won't mind either, that's for sure," I said, jokingly.

Ann grew pensive. "I want to coax Roxie out of Number Eleven. I want her closer to me. What if that man comes back? I don't feel good about her way down at the other end of the resort, especially with Caprice not here."

"She seems pretty big on her privacy. I doubt she'd move, especially if you said it was for her safety." I wanted to confess to Ann that the man in question was not prying open the door—that he was not with Roxie by accident. But I could feel the heat from Roxie's glare on the back of my head and thought better of it.

"No, you're right, I know you're right. She would never do it." Ann looked down at Number Eleven. "You had to go and make it bigger, and the new deck, too—you had to make it the nicest place here." Ann took another long draw off her cigarette and coughed again.

That night, after a late dinner, Roxie joined us around the fire and brought two bottles of wine, one cabernet and one sauvignon blanc. She deftly popped both corks with a corkscrew she pulled from her back pocket and set them on the picnic table along with a stack of plastic cups. Crickets chirped in unison as shadows cloaked Palisade Point. Roxie chose the white and downed her cup with one swallow, then filled it back up again. She was uncharacteristically somber, but when she noticed my bandage, she asked about my knuckles. Ann sipped a cup of red and was far away, gazing at twinkling stars against the inky sky. I added two chunks of wood to the fire and it came back to life. After a few minutes, Roxie abruptly rose, grabbed the half-full bottle of sauvignon blanc by the neck, and slinked down to Number Eleven. Ann watched her sister in the firelight until she disappeared into the night. We heard the cabin door bang shut.

"Can I ask you something Ann?"

"Sure."

"What happened to Roxie's leg?"

Ann looked at me quizzically, like it was none of my business.

"She got burned as a kid. Why?"

"She has quite a scar."

"She was eight. A boy was chasing her with a snake and she was running and looking backward and tripped and fell into a pile of hot coals. She had to stay in the hospital for a month with a skin graft. My Mom was so upset she cried. Dad shook the boy with both hands and later had to apologize to the parents. It was the only time I saw him angry like that."

"I shouldn't have asked," I said, picturing the discolored patch of skin below her knee.

"It was bad. It got infected and she was in bed the rest of the summer with my Mom tending to her. We called it the Summer of No Fun. We had the room you're in. She was in the bottom bunk. Every night, she woke up in such pain that Mom came in to give her an aspirin and stroke her forehead."

TWENTY

Ann was sitting alone on a green lawn chair on Roxie's smallish deck. She was primed to make her plea for Roxie to change cabins to Number Two, next door. Ann wasn't confident and knew that Roxie would come back with a snide comment about boundaries that would make her whole idea sound juvenile and absurd. Still, the incident with the man haunted Ann; she kept replaying it with terrible outcomes until she made herself nauseous. Ann had always complained about Roxie's free spirit and her selective rejection of facts, but she knew Roxie was her life's rudder, especially now. Roxie had always been the stubborn object for Ann to push against, and the tension somehow produced a stabilizing effect. Even as a small child, Ann obeyed her parents and dutifully followed the rules, but posed her important life questions to her older sister. Roxie always gave an answer, sometimes unsettling ones, for young Ann.

"Want coffee?" Roxie asked from inside the screen

door, toweling her long black hair.

"I would, if it's ready," Ann answered cautiously with her stomach churning.

Roxie returned with two cups of steaming coffee, wearing white cut-offs and a teal tee shirt, her long black hair falling loosely on her shoulders. They exchanged light small talk about groceries and Caprice. Roxie moved on to an evaluation of Owen's work performance, which surprised Ann with its positivity, specifically noting the excellent reconstruction of her cabin, Number Eleven. The carpet and tile were finished and Roxie said that it was the first time she ever lived in a brand new house. Ann hesitated to initiate a new conversation.

"How's our account?" Roxie asked.

"We're still pinched for cash," Ann began. "I told that to Owen. He offered to work for free for a while."

"Problem solved." Roxie was semi-serious.

"I told him it wasn't fair—that Dad wouldn't respect that."

Roxie sipped her coffee and looked out over Superior wistfully. She watched a hawk dive from high above the treetops and soar to the sky with a squirming field mouse in its talons.

"Roxie, would you ever consider giving up Number Eleven and moving next to me?"

"Why the hell would I do that?"

"I'll just be honest with you. The break-in terrified me. I can't stop thinking about what could've happened. Caprice isn't here much in the summer and I feel like you're vulnerable at the other end of the resort all alone. You always leave your windows open."

"Little sis, I am just fine where I am. You need to stay in your lane."

"I don't like it. Owen could've gotten hurt too. Can you for once think about people other than yourself?" Ann slid into precipitous territory challenging Roxie, and her back stiffened.

Roxie stayed quiet, looking thoughtfully at the big water.

"Well?" Ann prodded nervously.

"The man you're so worried about. The one at my door. He's a septic inspector for Cook County."

"What are you talking about?"

"He looked at our septic system in May. It failed inspection. He was going to shut us down going into Memorial Day." Roxie was direct, unapologetic, looking Ann in the eye.

"You talked him out of it?"

"Yeah, by fucking him. Twice."

Ann recoiled, slowing down Roxie's words in her head. *What did she say?* Her face lost color and her lip twitched. She spilled a little coffee over the brim and it burned against her thigh. *It can't be true.* Ann got up and backed away. She stepped off the low deck into the grass and walked slowly back to her cabin with her head down. She dumped out her coffee on the lawn.

"Had to do it, Ann. Had to be done," Roxie shouted at her sister. "You're welcome, by the way. Go back and play house with Owen."

Ann turned and shouted back through tears. "There was nothing you had to do. Don't you dare blame me. Ever."

Ann went inside and closed her bedroom door. She lay down on her bed slowly. She wanted only to see her parents, Ed and Marie, sitting on the edge of the bed and knowing just what to say to soothe the vice-like pain in her chest. How she wished they could be with her now, assuring her that this searing bit of horror would soon dissolve into insignificance. Ann was drenched in shame for a sin she had not perpetrated. She feared it would never wash off her. What would Caprice do? What would Owen think if he knew the truth? Owen assaulted the man and broke his nose. How did the man explain his mangled nose to his wife, if he had one? Or his children? What if he returned to Palisade in a rage? Ann's brain convulsed and she couldn't order her thoughts. Plumbing woes were overshadowed by a new, looming uncertainty, it seemed.

Ann would never again be able to visit her father alongside Roxie. Her dad, even in his compromised condition, would detect the space between them and that would be a bad way to leave the world.

That night Ann had a dream. In her dream she awoke floating in water. There was nothing but water; the whole Earth was a smooth ball of it. She looked around in every direction, scanning the horizon, but there was nothing to see. She dove underwater and discovered the eleven familiar cabin rooftops at Palisade Point. She could hear pounding coming from inside the cabins. She tried to swim down but it was too deep and piercing pain stabbed her ears. She popped back above the water's surface and woke up in her bed not knowing what was real.

TWENTY-ONE

It dawned on me that I hadn't driven the Camry in more than a week and it was low on gas, so I set out for my favorite lonely gas station in Schroeder, where I had happily camped out the night before starting work at Palisade Point. It was a breezy morning and grayish, but already there were pillars of light breaking through the blanket of clouds and I was optimistic the day would clear. Weather, more than anything else, affected the sequence of my daily chores, so I made a habit of watching the sky. I didn't need a weather report, just observation and experience.

I recognized the grizzled manager through the glass, the man who had graciously allowed me to park overnight back in April. The place was teeming with ebullient fishermen loading buckets of live bait into the beds of their pickup trucks. They were in stampede mode, so I parked off to the side and waited my turn. There was an event of some sort going on down the road. I could see a white vinyl tent billowing in the breeze. Cars slowed down to pull in, and a crowd was milling about under the square canopy. The manager recognized me and gave me a wizened squint that seemed benevolent.

"Still on the job?" he asked.

"Going okay so far, I think, thanks for asking. Can I add a coffee to my gas?" I filled a paper cup with hazelnut coffee, the only option available. The dispenser sputtered and spewed grounds, so I had to stop at half a cup.

"Coffee's free."

"Even better. I'm ahead for the day."

More fishermen came through the door looking for live bait, so I stepped aside, sipped my coffee and paused to reflect. Palisade Point, so far at least, wasn't at all like the jobs I'd in the past. In fact, it didn't seem like much a job at all. I worked at my own pace. I admired the place. I liked being around the women. And I felt a twinge of humility when I tinkered in Ed Martini's big garage. The humility grounded me, made me feel on good terms with the man who was no longer there. I put down cash on the counter and the manager spread out the bills, adding them up on his fingers.

"What's the deal down the road?" I asked. "Looks like a wedding or something."

"Groundbreaking for the new resort. Sturgeon Shores.

I hope it's good for me, but my luck they'll probably put in their own gas and grocery. These new operators want you to spend all your money right on the premises. Greedy people they are. One of them was in here the other day complaining about my pumps. Not a very nice fellow, if you ask me. Cook County says my pumps are too close to the road, but I'm grandfathered in. When they go, I go too," he said, shaking his head. He slid back a dollar bill.

I drove south to get a closer look at Sturgeon Shores. There was nobody in my rearview mirror, so I slowed to a crawl. There was a platform underneath the tent with a podium and a microphone. A man was speaking to a group of thirty or forty well-dressed people, most of them seated in white folding chairs and a few standing off to the side. I rolled down my window to listen but couldn't make out what he was saying; it was garbled at a distance. He looked familiar, and I had the idea that he was the same guy who had stopped earlier to talk to Ann. There was a black BMW parked with other fancy cars, and that confirmed my suspicion. He gestured in a couple of directions and then pointed back to large pictures mounted on easels on the stage. A wind gust caught one of the easels, sent it sailing. A young woman in a short black skirt and impossibly high heels scampered off to retrieve it.

Behind the tent, four enormous earth movers stood

motionless and silent, silhouetted against Superior, arranged in two neat rows like a Roman phalanx. They had stripped the site clean, exposing the earth below, probably ten or more acres, its flora and fauna scraped away with nothing left but gentle contours of raw soil. A few isolated pines had been spared and looked sad and naked in their new environment. An oncoming semi appeared in my rearview mirror so I hit the gas.

When I returned to Palisade Point, I had a mischievous inclination to poke around in the garage's endless inventory and sorted through a five-gallon bucket of miscellaneous hardware I found weeks ago under the workbench. There were hundreds of nuts and bolts, and I divided them up by size, using a dozen green glass Mason jars I also found under the workbench. It brought me back to Miller's Lake, as a kid. Back then, when I had the garage to myself, I pretended it was a hardware store with me as the proprietor. I imagined customers coming into my store with very specific requests, like No. 10 two-inch wood screws. I would expertly pull the right merchandise and put it out on the table. My Mason jars were about half filled with hardware when Caprice Wind startled me, standing behind me in the open garage door.

"Caprice? How long have you been there?"

"Just wanted to say thanks for the new shower, Owen. There's room for two. It's wonderfully nice."

"You're welcome. It wasn't that hard to install, to be honest."

Caprice was softer than Roxie, but just as unapologetic and utterly unafraid. I had the thought that nothing could pain her emotionally—that her soul floated on a long tether, somewhere out beyond such human frailties. Caprice abruptly spun a graceful pirouette, then pushed down her black shorts and underwear to waggle her bare brown butt at me. I was stunned when she turned back around for a full-frontal shimmy with her shorts still down. She pulled them back up and skipped away playfully, giggling at my expense. My face felt hot. I remembered when, at the age of twelve, I nervously peeled open my first *Playboy* centerfold, Miss December, revealing truths only snickered about by boys with more experience. Miss December's body had the same satiny tone as Caprice Wind's, and she wore nothing but a carefully placed white feather boa that I traced with my boyish fingertips, hoping it would fall away. The magazine was a major discovery inside my adoptive father's closet. I was looking for a blank notebook and found a *Playboy* instead. I put it back where I found it, handling the magazine with precision, treating it like a plutonium sample. Knowing it was in his closet felt as dangerous and unpredictable as a keg of dry gunpowder under my bed. I recovered from my trance and peered outside the garage. Caprice was already back inside Number Eleven.

I looked over at the colorful Titan Industries sign leaning against the far wall of the garage. There was rust accumulating along the bottom edge, no doubt the result of moisture in the floor slab, so it seemed prudent to mount it in a safer location. But it was heavy. I considered my options and chose a space on the wall across from the workbench. I needed to relocate a set of wooden shelves, which took no time. I dragged the massive Titan sign into position and chained a pully to a roof truss up in the garret. I fed a nylon rope through the pulley and attached it to the sign's center mounting hole. It was surprisingly easy work to raise the sign into place against the bare studs. I tied off the rope to the John Deere, got on a ladder, and drove a lag bolt through the center hole into a stud. I removed the rope and pulley, checked for level, and drove in four more lag bolts, top and bottom. Once mounted securely up on the wall, the Titan sign looked even bigger and more foreboding, looking down at me. Ed Martini would have approved.

TWENTY-TWO

The visage of Palisade Point in the distance was worthy of a picture postcard. Everywhere, my handiwork was in evidence. The grounds were tailored, finally free of eradicated stubborn weeds, and overseeded bare patches were coming up green. Number Eleven was restored, better than the original, and it nicely bookended one end of the resort. Pyramids of freshly split birch and oak were outside every door, and a fresh coat of yellow paint enlivened the buildings against the verdant landscape. The scene was bucolic but energized as well. Ann said the upcoming weekend was promising, with only Number Four left empty, which gave me more time to resolve the plumbing quandary, but I knew Fourth of July was fully booked and around the corner. I mulled over options to deal with pesky Number Four. I could always bunk in the garage and Ann could move in with Roxie, freeing up Number One for guests. An imperfect solution to be sure, but at least a possible Plan B. I wasn't thrilled to suggest such an extreme idea, so I kept it to myself for the time being. I intended to get a secret plumbing quote without telling Ann. That was my Plan A.

Aside from plumbing difficulties, my other challenge was filling my newfound free time. I had mastered the tasks of maintaining Palisade Point to the point where I finished everything quicker than before. Unoccupied time was a ubiquitous bogeyman for me and always proved corrosive to my mental state. My mind shifted to Grand Marais. It seemed a perfect day to visit the tiny bookstore I had seen near the harbor. I put a hold on the mission long enough to stop at Palisade Point to tell Ann where I was going. Surprisingly, she asked to ride along, and that was a welcome development. She changed clothes and plopped into the front seat of the Camry. We weren't very far along when Ann excitedly patted the dash with both hands and sat up straight.

"There's Lutsen Lodge."

"What ?"

"Lutsen. My favorite memory is the Christmas Eve Mom and Dad took us to Lutsen for dinner. Since it was Christmas, Dad said we could order anything on the menu, dessert included, and we never got to order dessert. That just didn't happen. Mom stared a hole in him. He was thrifty, but she was tight. Dad was laughing, full of cheer and telling the waitress stories he made up about us girls.

He told her we were let out of jail for Christmas, but we had to go right back to solitary after dinner."

Ann was reveling in the memory, almost levitating, as we drove by the big timber Lutsen Lodge sign.

"Your dad was quite the jokester."

"I remember rubbing the edge of the tablecloth between my fingers. It was so white and so soft."

"And you managed to serve your time and get out of solitary." I laughed with Ann. I checked my speedometer with a highway patrol coming at us from the opposite direction. Ann quietly watched out the window and I considered what it must feel like to know one's parents, to hold onto a collection of shared moments, to keep alive the tales of tenderness and love, to be encouraged, years later, by the vision of facial features around the dinner table, Marie's slender neck and Ed's nose, which was also Roxie's, to know the lasting affections that gradually accrue from living under a shared roof. I knew none of that, and I was tormented by an achy hole in my heart.

Ann purred with her eyes closed and sank into the car seat. "We went back to Lutsen every Christmas Eve. The low ceilings and log walls. It was like having Christmas in a giant hollowed-out tree; the room smelled like cinnamon and was lit by a hundred flickering candles, more like fireflies hovering over the tables. The silverware sparkled.

The frosty moon was harmless outside, reflecting off Superior."

"You and Roxie ever go back?"

"Not after Mom passed away. I don't think Dad wanted to go back without her. Too hard for him. He never mentioned it again and we just left it alone."

"Maybe you should go with me sometime? I mean, I've never seen the lodge. Always wanted to, but I was always on the way somewhere."

"I'll think about it," Ann said, sleepily.

"Roxie's welcome too."

"That first Christmas Eve, Roxie and I were dozing in the backseat on the way back to Palisade. Dad started yelling for us to wake up. We looked over the front seat to see lights at Palisade. He strung lights on all the cabins and they were all lit up. It looked like Santa's workshop at the North Pole. Red, green, yellow, blue, the whole yard was covered in new snow and glowed. Roxie and I started screaming and bouncing on the car seat. I was convinced Santa Claus was real. Mom and Dad were singing "Jingle Bells" at the top of their lungs. Our ears hurt but we didn't care. I will never forget that night."

We found Gideon Books and it was right where I remembered. The bookstore was a cluttered, musty grotto, full of dangling bare bulbs. An enormous antique brass cash register was intriguingly ornate. It was the kind of place I loved to forage through, but Ann's expression communicated less enthusiasm. She politely offered to shop at a clothing store down the street while I dug for my next read. She told me to take my time. I forgot to bring along my book on medieval armor to trade but figured it wasn't worth much anyway. There appeared to be a system to the shelves, with subjects written in Sharpie on notecards taped in place. In a rear alcove, surrounded by bookcases, I came upon "Of Local Interest" and thought that might yield a gem. I pawed through several stacks of books until the artwork on one cover caught my attention. It was a pen and ink, expressively drawn, and simple in design. Two canoeists were maneuvering through a narrow whitewater passage, partially obscured by a veil of skinny, leafy birches. The two men were tight-lipped and focused on the water ahead, with firm, two-handed grips on their paddles. It was called The Lonely Land by Sigurd Olson. There was a black-and-white photo of the author inside the dust jacket. He stared back at me, stern and weathered, with heavy-lidded eyes and a hint of condescension. His face alone convinced me that he was the real deal, a modern voyageur, and that Lonely Land was worth my time.

Ann and I stopped for ice cream at a miniature two-story house that was brightly painted with dormers and balconies perfectly scaled for people three feet tall. Inside the service window on the side of the house, two normal-sized teenage girls took orders for ice cream cones and sundaes. With our treats in hand, we strolled along the curved stony beach at Grand Marais harbor. Gray stones were plentiful, ancient droplets from a primordial volcano, rubbed round and smooth by eons of grinding against each other in the big water. Ann hooked her little finger around mine as we walked. We encountered a flock of meandering gulls who were pecking away at scraps of bread thrown by a group of young children who stood by watching. Our intrusion sent the birds aloft and shrieking. The little girl in the middle of the group put her hands on her hips and frowned at us. Ann tried not to laugh.

TWENTY-THREE

That night I slept with Ann for a second time. It was at my initiation this time instead of hers, although not without some provocation from her. Roxie was overnight in Duluth with Caprice and that emboldened me. I waited to shower until Ann was finished in the bathroom so she wouldn't run short of hot water. I was used to taking cold showers, and they didn't bother me much. After my shower, I dried off and wrapped myself in a thin but still serviceable towel. Ann waited for me outside the bathroom door in her apricot robe. It fell open and she was nude underneath.

"I'm going to bed," Ann said with hopeful eyes.

I glanced down the hall toward my empty room. A corner of my bed was visible through the open door, neatly made since morning. I heard the friction click of an igniting match from Ann's room just as her light went off. Her doorway was framed in warm candlelight, transformed into a portal to a feminine lair. A siren's call. It was time for a decision, I thought, one that might bring along various consequences and complications, so naturally I scratched at the back of my wet head. *Do I pull on boxers out of respect or does that scream inexperience to a girl like Ann Martini?* I dropped my towel and proceeded into Ann's room fully exposed. It was cavernous in low light and Ann was on her side, half covered by a sheet. I was reasonably confident about my body, but still recovering from a shower that finished cool and my heart was racing. There were three translucent candles on her dresser arranged in a triangle, the trio of flames swaying hypnotically. My eyes adjusted and I moved toward her bed with small steps. Her tantalizingly female form was fully revealed. Her robe was draped over a chair, looking deflated and useless. I slid in, facing her, and she drew my body tight against hers, kissed me on my mouth, and touched my face.

"This is a perfect ending to the day, and a surprise," I whispered in her ear.

"Maybe for you, but I've been thinking about this for over a week. Owen, you're so cold. I ran you out of water," Ann answered, then she pulled up a blanket over us both.

"Sorry." The warmth of her body caused my skin to tingle.

"You won't stay cold very long with me."

There were qualities about Ann that were so foreign

to me that I had to question the value of my prior experience with women. I was not in the lead here. I thrust myself into this intimacy without any useful training, no preparation or even a whisper of a parallel moment that could guide my behavior. Ann trusted herself. I had to think things through in advance and convince myself to act. Honestly, there have so many times in my life when I've wandered without a plan, distrusting my own ambitions and aimlessly waiting for the path of least resistance to appear. Ann was like water trickling through a crevasse in a boulder. She filled every notch and groove and waited for a good freeze. The water would overcome the rock, without any effort, all in good time.

"What are we listening to?" I asked. There was a calm melody coming from a shadowy corner. My lips still quivered from the first soft contact. Ann slowly slid her soft hand across my chest, stopping just below my navel. She scratched me lightly with her nails.

"John Coltrane. You like him?"

"I do." I reached for Ann's bare hip. She intercepted my hand and tucked it between her thighs. The remaining chill fled my body.

Her exquisite form was blessedly familiar from our first night together. But now, without the obstacles of pajamas and good manners, her physical perfection was electric. Her warm, silky legs offered no resistance or modesty. Her thighs were tender with a firmness underneath that produced a lump in my throat. With the lazy jazz melody flowing, I released the last strand of residual anxiety that clung to me. She sighed audibly. We moved in unison, fluidly intersected, caressing each other in the undulating light of pine-scented candles and Coltrane. I didn't want it to ever end, but I had little control over that. Ann was in no hurry either and she kept kissing me with her fingers tugging on my damp hair.

I woke up in the middle of a moonless night and blew out the candles. Melted wax had run over the sides and onto the top of the dresser. Ann was curled in a ball, sleeping like a bear cub. Pleasing smoke wafted up from the extinguished candles in the dark. I added another blanket to cover the two of us and held Ann until morning.

At first light, Ann was already up and in the kitchen. The familiar clinking and tinny sounds suggested muffins and coffee. I was reluctant to make a naked retreat to my room for clothes, but I didn't have a choice. Ann immediately noticed my naked backside and whistled at me. I pulled on jeans and a sweatshirt and glanced out of my bedroom window to see if Roxie had returned early from Duluth. I thought it more likely she would visit Ed on her way home. Her VW wasn't there, so I was in the clear. I had a gnawing concern that the intuitive Roxie would see it on my face, written boldly across my forehead, telling her all about last night with Ann. She would stare me up and down until my bluff collapsed. I wasn't a particularly good liar. The truth was bound to come out eventually, I knew, because I would never have the willpower to refuse Ann again, whether Roxie was at Palisade Point or not. I decided to bury that psychological land mine deep enough to enjoy breakfast with Ann. The muffins were filled with marble-sized fresh blueberries, steaming with melted butter on top.

"The candles melted on your dresser. I'll get the wax off with a plastic spatula." I started off the conversation deliberately innocent, unsure of morning-after protocol. *How do you return to the world after exploring a mysterious fold in the universe like Ann Martini's bedroom?* I dreaded the loss of her scent on my skin, so I put off my morning shower.

"Look Owen, I need you to know that I don't expect anything from you. Nothing's changed except that we both needed attention at the same time. When that happens…" Ann's voice trailed off.

"What?"

"I don't question it. I don't give guilt any power in my life. You shouldn't either."

"I won't."

"Did you like it?" Ann grinned at me.

"I won't ever forget it."

And there it was. The Martini pedigree. The animal purposefulness. Simultaneous pangs of uncertainty and ecstasy, two emotions that should be mutually exclusive, crashed together inside me like cymbals and rendered me foggy. At Ann's encouragement, I trusted her instincts, not mine. Sun seeped through the blinds and filled the kitchen with pink morning light from across the big water to the east. My memory of Ann's bed slowly receded like a gauzy dream that fades upon waking. I craved solitude to carve it into my brain more permanently. I heard the shower start and tried to remember everything about Ann's body. I lingered at the table, dunking my muffin in my coffee. The birds outside were joyous in their flitting.

TWENTY-FOUR

I toted my new Sigurd Olson book with me to the Blue Heron, thinking I would show it to Dean Aker and see if he knew anything about the author. Already, at midmorning, the lobby was bustling with four queues of impatient guests waiting to check in early. The double doors to Keegan's pub were closed, but the lights were on, and I could hear the low rumble of a vacuum cleaner. I cadged a coffee from the concierge and made my way out on the sprawling deck that looked out on Superior. The lake was catching the morning sun in animated white streaks dancing across the surface, with only the gentlest of breezes coming from the southwest. It was mind-boggling to think that the Blue Heron was about to be dwarfed by the new wonder down the coast, Sturgeon Shores. I knew from experience that real Sturgeon existed in Lake Superior, so the name had some credibility. Outside on the deck there were dozens of matching white tables with red umbrellas covering the long, wide deck. Its lakeside railing was constructed of tempered glass with a rail cap made of polished stainless steel, much like a modern cruise ship. Given the bustling lobby, the deck was strangely empty. It felt mildly criminal for me to impersonate a paying customer, sipping my stolen coffee and enjoying the view for free. I took another sip, then I paged through my new book, *The Lonely Land*, turned it over and back in my hands. It was weighty with a straight spine.

The dust jacket provided information. The author, Olson, was an accomplished outdoorsman. He was born in Chicago in 1899 and went on to earn multiple degrees from the University of Wisconsin, with far-ranging interests in geology, animal ecology, and biology. It also said he taught biology for several years at Ely Junior College, where he later served as dean. *Lonely Land* was his third book, and there were many others to follow. There was a chronological list of Olson's books, all with titles that included some connection to the Quetico-Superior wilderness. The pen and ink sketch on the cover that caught my eye back at Gideon Books was one of many drawings throughout the book by the same artist. In my opinion, they were exceptionally well done, each one portraying the theme of the coming chapter. The artist's name was Francis Lee Jaques. I'd ask Dean about him too.

I read Chapter One under the shade of a red umbrella

and was amused by my failed attempts to pry into the book on medieval armor. It never took root with me. A dozen pages in I was already captivated by *The Lonely Land,* and there was likely no better place in the world than Lake Superior to read this adventure tale. The story had to do with Olson and his comrades setting out to undertake the treacherous navigation of the Churchill River, from western Saskatchewan to Manitoba, following a water route that was originally followed by the earliest voyageurs.

When I looked up from my book, the deck at the Blue Heron had nearly filled up with boisterous families. Young, skirted waitresses scurried around, scratching down lunch orders and handing out color crayons to the kids. The deck vibrated noticeably, and that turned my attention back to the intractable plumbing issue at Palisade Point. I had a bad feeling about it. Ann would be insulted, for certain, if I hired a plumber on my own. I didn't want to jeopardize our fledgling intimacy. I would just have to manage the problem, blow out the pipes the best I could in between reservations to get through the season.

I was getting hungry watching the plates coming out from the kitchen, so I wandered back inside to Keegan's, where the doors were now propped wide open and there was an empty stool at the end of the bar. Dean Aker was behind the bar with his back to me, wiping down the fancy brass beer taps.

Dean spun around and beamed with pride. "Hello Mr. Owen."

"Hey Dean, are you working again?" I said, knowing that he liked it when people acknowledged his tenacious work ethic. I was the same way.

"What can I say? The governor wants his money. What can I get for you?"

"I'll try another Reuben, and a rum and coke." I looked around at the immaculate restaurant. It was filling up quickly. I heard Dean smack his lips.

"You're a bartender's nightmare—never the same drink twice. Rum and coke it is. What's that there?"

"I bought this in Grand Marais, at Gideon Books. It's by an outdoorsman named Sigurd Olson. Hear of him?"

"Hear of him? Good God, he's legend up here. Used to live in Ely. I think I remember he died snowshoeing in Ely back in the 1980s. He was pretty old by then. That was a long time ago, you know." Dean held up the book in front of his nose and squinted. "He wrote lots of books about the Boundary Waters, and Superior. I heard him interviewed on the Duluth radio station once. Knowledgeable man as I recall, with a growly voice."

"Which one was your favorite?" I was hoping Dean would endorse *The Lonely Land*.

"Never read a one. I'm not a reader. But they're all

over the Blue Heron if you look around." Dean dropped the book on the bar and high-stepped to the kitchen with my order clenched in his beefy hand.

TWENTY-FIVE

Two days in front of the Fourth of July weekend, there was a trace of humidity in the air, and also, for me at least, considerable apprehension. I strolled the quiet grounds, which would become a cacophony of cars and families very soon. By Thursday night, every cabin would be filled with an influx of new guests, the next wave, so to speak, and Ann said most of them come for every Fourth. One set of parents met at Palisade as children, later married, and now bring their own. I wondered how long they would all choose to bypass the amenities of the Blue Heron for a walk back in time at Palisade Point. Maybe it was an emotional strand of continuity for them that their children didn't yet appreciate. That's my speculation. Still, all summer long it was hard to ignore kids wandering toward the road to get a better look at the indoor waterpark at the Blue Heron. I expected the young ones silently pined for the waterpark, but marshmallows were marshmallows, and that was a saving grace when mixed with a campfire.

Caprice Wind agreed to spend the weekend with Roxie at Palisade, despite her aversion to too many congregated White people. Roxie insisted. She had a full slate of cave tours booked each day, and she needed Caprice's help. I saw Ann bring out a green stoneware bowl that was heaped with steaming contents, so I figured it was lunch. She came back again with plates, silverware, glasses, and an open bottle of chardonnay. She smiled when I sat down and took a fork full straight from the bowl. We got settled in at the picnic table. I could hear her music through the screen door, soft piano with a gentle saxophone.

"I hope you like this. Pretty simple fare for us today." Ann was proud of stretching groceries, I could tell, and she was good at it.

"It smells incredible, what's in it?"

"Wild rice, jasmine rice, white onions from the garden, a little curry, soy sauce, and two kinds of wild mushrooms fried in butter." She ticked off the ingredients on her fingers.

In other words, it cost next to nothing to prepare. I looked over the sticky glob on my fork. "You know your wild mushrooms, right? I mean, the edible ones from the ones that you only eat once?" I asked casually but waited for the answer.

"Yes, Owen, I do. They grow uplands around here.

I've been picking the same ones in the same places since I was a kid. Mom used them in everything. Dad loved wild mushrooms on his eggs in the morning." Ann turned her head toward a framed picture of Ed Martini on the kitchen counter.

"Only one way to find out," I said morbidly, like responding to a death sentence.

"Well?"

"It's very good." I took another bite and savored it. "It tastes like the forest floor in the way I always thought steamed mussels tasted of the ocean bottom."

"Are you trying to sound like a food critic?" Ann asked rhetorically, smirking back at me. "But I don't mind if you only offer compliments."

I scooped out more of the rice dish on my plate, then snatched up a dark brown mushroom from the bowl.

"I checked all the toilets and drains, and they're all flowing, including Four and Five, although Five backed up a little on me. I think we should get through the weekend, fingers crossed."

"Really Owen? While we're eating?" Ann looked at her food and frowned.

"Thought you'd want to know. Just information. Nothing more needs to be said. We'll change the subject."

"Caprice gets here in the morning. We can't count much on them this weekend with the kayaking they've got arranged. Can you put out the flag?"

"Sure. Everything else is ready. The cabins are good to go," I said, doing my best to calm Ann.

She looked over at my rebuilt Number Eleven. It was bigger and better, with a lakeside deck, new kitchen and bath, new windows. It was a witness in many ways to Ed Martini's construction skills and his native sense of landscape. It was one of the most satisfying projects in my life. I delighted in finding Ed's hand sketches tacked up in the garage, showing the layout of the original resort when he and Marie bought the place, and his ideas for additional cabins. When he was done, the overall aesthetic of the property was enhanced by the careful placement of the additional structures. It was a masterful plan.

"What are we listening to today?" I asked.

"This one's Miles Davis."

"Different than Coltrane, simpler I think, but you're the expert. I never listened to any jazz until I got here. Do I seem a little more sophisticated?"

"It makes me feel safe," Ann said thoughtfully, ignoring my question.

"If jazz makes you feel safe, I'm surprised you ever turn it off."

"Owen, that man you punched in the face."

"What about him?"

Ann looked away. "He wasn't trying to break in. He's

a county inspector. He was going to shut us down because our septic system isn't working." Ann looked back at me.

"What are you trying to say?"

"Roxie bought us time. He agreed to delay the order to shut us down. Owen, she slept with him. I didn't want to tell you."

It made sense and fit the picture, but the implications were many. For one, I assaulted a county employee. An unsavory man, but an innocent one. I shattered his nose and he didn't lay a hand on me. It seemed a step too far for Roxie, but apparently not. No amount of my cleaning drain lines would repair a failed system. "Okay." It was all I could say and hardly enough.

Ann started sobbing. "He's probably married. What an evil man. You don't think he'll come back, do you? How does she keep this from Caprice?"

"Come back here? I doubt it." I rubbed the scar on my knuckles.

"You can't ever let Roxie know I told you. No one can ever know, especially Caprice. This never happened. The thought of it makes me feel sick."

"I understand."

I stayed up late reading, and Ann seemed entirely unavailable to me. I could faintly detect music coming from her room, a low bass beat. Her door was shut and her lights were out. I managed to stay up long enough to read several chapters of *The Lonely Land*. I was so intrigued by one passage that I scribbled it down inside the back cover along with the page number. It read:

> *Old-timers and Indians have this sort of sixth sense about the weather, a sense above and beyond barometers, something learned through a hundred thousand years or more of watching the skies. Dormant among those who have lived too long in cities with shelters impervious to storms, it can become alive and reliable with experience.*

I had this sixth sense, too, born of experience. I sensed a storm building.

TWENTY-SIX

A light rain started to fall just as the first car drove into Palisade Point. The morning sky was overcast and even ominous out over the lake, where wispy dark clouds were twirling in opposite directions. The blackish clouds danced together a bit, hinting at an infantile tornado, but then went their separate ways. Soon the skies began to lighten, as so often happens on Superior, but the light rain showed no signs of letting up. On arrival, three boys exploded out of the parked car, running in circles out on the wet grass, oblivious to the falling rain, screaming nonsense and pretending to be airplanes. The parents were quite the opposite. Weary from the road, they were focused on getting inside their cabin with damp grocery bags and suitcases. I watched from my dry perch, sitting on a wooden stool inside Ed Martini's open garage. The raindrops pinged off the corrugated roof; a few struck so hard I checked the ground for hail but there was nothing. A good rain like this brought out the ineffable aroma of minerals hiding in the earth. The mother waved the boys inside, but they ignored her calls. By midafternoon we had seven cabins accounted for and everyone was warm and dry. The rain continued.

Roxie and Caprice pulled in with their trailer full of kayaks. Roxie spotted me in the garage and looked irritated. She walked over, leaving Caprice to unload.

"The last group was a bunch of entitled shits who complained nonstop about getting rained on. I cut it short and they crabbed about that too. We're done for the day and Caprice wants to go home. Everything okay here?"

"Yeah, people just started checking in." I noticed Ann in her hooded windbreaker delivering a box of Eskimo Pies. She reminded me at breakfast that the Fourth of July is the break-even point for the season. She chatted for a minute with the new arrivals, saw us in the garage, and walked over.

"Damn rain. Why this weekend?" Ann squinted skyward.

"It'll pass, Ann," Roxie said over her shoulder and went back to Number Eleven.

"Just the first day," I said. "I see you're giving them away now."

"What?"

"Eskimo Pies."

"I'm compensating for the rain, that's all."

"The rain won't affect cocktail hour, so there's nothing to worry about." I saw the dad carry a box of liquor inside.

"The Ashmans in Number Three want some dry wood for the Franklin stove. The stacks out front are too wet. Everybody's going to want dry wood to burn indoors tonight. Get that done, okay?" Ann was humorless and direct. I felt like an employee for the first time at Palisade Point. I looked Ann in the eye, but she was unrelenting.

"I'll take care of it. Ashmans first." It was a good thing I always anticipated rain and had a whole cord of split oak covered with waterproof tarps behind the garage. I tied off a bundle for each cabin, wrapping them all in poly. I heard Roxie's VW start up and drive away. There was nothing much for them to do at Palisade Point, anyway. It was an inside day for everyone.

By nine o'clock the night sky was inky, with intermittent flashes of lightning and a windless downpour. The cabins were full, all nine of them, Two through Ten. I grabbed an umbrella and went outside to inspect the grounds with a flashlight. There were miniature streams running haphazardly in between some of the cabins down to the ditch alongside Highway 61. I didn't think flooding was an issue given our sloped terrain, but there was a concerning volume of water running toward the road. Our looping gravel drive had washed away in spots, and that would need attention as soon as things dried. All of the cabin windows glowed, except for Roxie's, hard to see in the darkness, but for lightning flashes. I concluded that Roxie chose to stay with Caprice in Duluth rather than drive back through the weather.

Finally satisfied that the storm no longer posed a serious threat, I retreated inside to find Ann stretched out on the couch with a bourbon and ice high ball on the end table next to her. She was wearing soft pink underwear and one of my sweatshirts.

"Owen, I've been a bitch today."

"It's okay, Ann. You know better than I do that no two trips to the North Shore are ever the same. You get what you get up here. These families will be talking about this storm for years to come. They're inside playing Monopoly instead of sitting by the fire pit. There's smoke coming out of the chimneys. Tomorrow's a new day. Let's just see what it brings, okay?"

Ann sat up to take a drink. A thunder crack sounded close.

"Okay," she said. "Drink with me. I'll put on Etta James. She goes well with bourbon."

She stretched and got up with a flash of her pert rump. She and Roxie shared Ed and Marie's determination genes. It's what delivered the family to Palisade Point in the first place.

There was a startling bang on the front door that made

Ann jump. It was followed by aggressive knocking, or more like a succession of open-handed slaps on the door. I looked out the window to see a man in a hat and rain jacket. I opened the door to see Eugene Underdahl, who I had met for the first time earlier in the day. He and his wife were the second to arrive after the Ashmans, bringing with their two young grandchildren all the way from Rochester, in southeastern Minnesota. That was a long journey for one day. They were in Number Five, and that was a red flag for me.

"Mr. Underdahl," Ann said from behind the couch, caught off guard without clothes. "What's wrong?"

"Our Benny took a tub and when he flushed the toilet the tub filled up with sewage. It's a stinking mess over there."

"Oh no," Ann said through her hands.

"I had to stuff a towel under the door to keep the stench out of the living room. We can't stay there," Eugene Underdahl shouted at us through the rain. "What are you going to do about it?"

"Please come in out of the rain," Ann stammered.

"No."

"Mr. Underdahl, I'm so sorry," Ann said with a terrified expression. "We are all full up. But I will make some calls right away and get you in somewhere nearby."

"I'll give you five minutes," Underdahl said and

slammed the door behind him.

"Owen, this is bad."

I knew it was bad. Ann frantically flipped through the pages of her binder until she got to a list of several resorts nearby. It was probably not unusual to move guests back and forth due to occasional overbooking or extended stays, but I couldn't imagine many options on the Fourth of July.

She started dialing her phone and I went to my bedroom to give her space. Her voice was squeaky, like a woman on the verge of tears. Eventually she came into my room, dejected, and sat down on the bed.

"What can we do?" Ann asked, teary. "There's nothing."

"Roxie's in Duluth. Let's put them in Number Eleven and see if Roxie can stay down there through the weekend."

"She won't like it. She would never share her cabin with strangers."

"It may be the only option," I said. I could tell Ann was thinking it through.

"What happens when the grandkids find something adult in one of the bedroom drawers?"

I hadn't accounted for that mortifying possibility. Ann had a point. Number Eleven wouldn't work.

"How about here?" I suggested. "They can take our

cabin for the weekend and we'll stay in Roxie's. Besides, maybe it'll be just one night. We'll call around again in the morning to check on cancellations."

"Will you go and tell him?" Ann pleaded.

"Sure."

I sloshed along in the rain, not too eager to the deliver the news. It wasn't much of a silver lining. Underdahl was waiting for me, holding the door open a few inches, glaring back at me with flinty eyes. I caught a piercing whiff of feces and gagged a little. The stench was intolerable. He asked me in and I had no choice. Mrs. Underdahl and the grandchildren were huddled together on a recliner in the corner of the living room. I saw a towel jammed under the bathroom door. The kids were crying uncontrollably and she was stroking their hair.

"What do we do?" Underdahl demanded in no uncertain terms.

"We would like to put you up in the main cabin, our cabin. It's bigger and very comfortable. We'll just need to get a few things put together, no more than fifteen minutes. We'll spend the night in Ann's sister's cabin. She's away for the weekend."

"You expect us to move these kids, in their pajamas, and all of our things to your cabin in this thunderstorm? Where you live? We've had about enough of this."

"I don't know what else to offer."

Underdahl looked me over and was straining to compose himself.

"This trip with our grandkids to Palisade Point was supposed to be very special."

"I know. I can't imagine…"

"Here's what we're going to do. You'll help me load up the car right now. You are refunding me one hundred percent, and that includes interest on the deposit I gave you twelve months ago. Twelve months! Ed Martini ran this place like a top, but boy have times changed. We'll bring two very disappointed young ones back home. Disgusting is what this is."

"I'm so sorry," I said apologetically.

Underdahl pointed at the bathroom door. "That kind of problem doesn't pop up out of nowhere. Be honest."

"We've had some trouble." I fell on my sword.

TWENTY-SEVEN

Miraculously, the intense rain, torrential in bursts, tapered off to a harmless warm drizzle by sunrise on the Fourth of July. Fireworks displays up and down the coast would have a chance, especially the big shows in Duluth and Grand Marais. The Blue Heron advertised its own fireworks on its massive electronic sign alongside Highway 61. I was looking forward to it. Dean Aker at the Heron told me that watching fireworks over Superior is like watching two shows at once, one in the air and another reflected on the water. The idea of watching the spectacle over the harbor in Grand Marais was enticing, but it was likely a dicey time to leave Ann alone at Palisade Point. Alternatively, the short walk to the Blue Heron might be the better option. She may even decide to tag along, and it would be a healthy distraction for an hour. She was taking the Underdahl situation hard.

Ann paid little attention to me as I soft-shoed through

the tomb-like kitchen. She was in her robe, flipping pages back and forth in her business binder. I was inclined to avoid a morning conversation with her anyway, but it was obvious that wasn't a concern. Instead, I figured it was a perfect opportunity to rake and repair the erosion along the edges of the drive. I poured myself a cup of strong, black coffee. Ann unfolded a wide ledger, full of columns, dates, and dollar figures. She studiously made marks in pencil with her right hand while punching buttons on a Casio calculator with her left. I silently slipped out the door to find the drizzle had stopped entirely. A family of five bubbled out of Number Two, right next door, all dressed for the day's activities, and they waved back at me appreciatively. They said they were on the way up to Grand Marais to spend the day and asked if I had any recommendations. I felt like a local when I suggested they try Gideon Books, where I'd found my Sigurd Olson gem. The middle child, a feisty red-headed girl about ten years old and wearing a striped one-piece, curled her lip and flashed me the peace sign.

The ground was spongy and there would be no point trying to mow for at least a couple of days. I would leave ruts all over and just clog up the John Deere. It would be a two-blader, I reckoned, since you could almost hear the grass grow after a rain like that. I would be cutting twice, once with the blade set high, and again with it down in proper position. The prospect of a full day of labor was reassuring. After three days of storms, it was good to see a more tranquil Superior. It was well-fed and must have wanted to rest.

By noon I was making progress with my gravel restoration and repair. I shoveled, raked, and tamped material back into place the best I could. Yet again, I benefited from Ed Martini's prescience. Deep in the brush behind the garage, there was a stockpile of gravel that Ed must have kept for storm repair. I allowed myself to think for a moment that Ed Martini left that gravel specifically for me. *Who really knows?* I carried out gravel in buckets and deposited the material in the remaining washed-out spots.

I could see the top of Ann's head through the window, so she was still agonizing over business receipts at the kitchen table. I had forgotten all about breakfast and was suddenly hungry. Ann wouldn't miss me if I disappeared for an early lunch at Keegan's down at the Blue Heron. I would wash up when I got there, rather than intrude on her again. Best leave her alone while she's working on the finances. Halfway to the Heron, I glanced back to take in Palisade Point, with its neatly arranged cabins with a backdrop of prehistoric rock that looked like a skyscraper to squinted eyes. A familiar VW flew by me. Roxie was home from Duluth and the sisters would need time to talk about the Underdahls, without me in the picture.

The Blue Heron was splitting at the seams. I waddled through the furious lobby, ringing with chatter and boiling energy that made me uncomfortable, like waking up in a Tiger cage. Fortunately, Keegan's was unusually subdued. But it was still early, and Dean Aker had just now opened the doors. He was busy stuffing dollar bills from his pants pocket into his glass tip jar, and good natured as always.

"Got to prime the pump Owen. Nobody tips an empty jar. Remember that."

"Makes sense to me," I said and climbed aboard a corner stool at the bar.

"So, you obviously survived the flood. I was thinking about you and the Martini girls during the storms, thinking that you should've been building yourself a little ark, just in case the three of you needed to save mankind," Dean said with a dramatic eye wink.

"We lost a cabin to a plumbing back-up, but otherwise we made it through. No damage other than a rutted driveway. We could use a few dry days though."

"Need a menu?"

"I do, and a stiff drink, honestly."

"Shoot."

"Double Jameson, neat. And no menu. I'll just have a hamburger and fries."

"Can you believe it? We are sold out of fries—I didn't

think it humanly possible. There were fifteen bags in the freezer just last Monday. How about tater tots instead?"

"Perfect, with ketchup, and Tabasco. Dean, I never asked you where you're from?"

"The whole Aker clan comes from the range. Eveleth. Biwabik. Aurora. Hoyt Lakes. There's a mess of us. We are known for strong backs and thick women," Dean Aker described his family tree with noticeable pride.

"Dean, I don't think you get to say that about women," I responded earnestly, but truthfully amused by his word choice.

"Why not? I've got the photo album to back it up. Skinny girls don't cut it on the Mesabi, pal. Hard work needs a sturdy frame. They don't come sturdier than the Aker women."

TWENTY-EIGHT

The color drained from Bill Trout's face as the excavation superintendent ticked off the reasons for stopping work. Trout's nostrils flared on his hawkish nose. He was exasperated by the man's tedious explanation. *Get to the point!* He couldn't follow the series of obtuse statements. Trout suffered a cognitive delay caused by the sight of halted equipment and contractors standing in a loose circle puffing on cigarettes. It was as if his ears were stuffed tight with cotton balls. Trout knew one thing for certain: the construction schedule had no padding to absorb any delays. *Why aren't you bastards working?* Trout swallowed hard and told the superintendent to get to the bottom line, in very simple terms. The superintendent started over and Trout realized that the work stoppage was complicated and maybe not temporary. The thought of opening the next investor's meeting of the Odin Forward partnership with bad news struck Trout as suicidal. He examined the expanse of land with its gaping hole in the earth, the place that would become Sturgeon Shores, an international destination resort. He heard riotous laughter coming from the water's edge, but it was a flock of white gulls squawking. He had never questioned his mental state during decades of slippery dealings, but now he was off balance and couldn't think clearly. The huge earth-moving machines were grunting and hissing their cool down, with the last puffs of black diesel smoke belching from the stacks. All that was left was the purr of a gas-fueled generator that fed the heat and lights in the job trailer. Men smoked with their hands in their pockets, waiting for instructions. They knew from experience that it was over.

Bill Trout implored the superintendent, "What does all this mean for the project?"

"It means we're done here, Trout. We will button up the site and go home. You'll spend all winter figuring this one out. Come and see us when you do, and we can ramp back up when you're sorted out." The superintendent was calm, with the measured confidence that is a natural by-product of performing the same task, over and over again, for many years.

"Where is it? I need to see it." Trout was insistent, frantic even.

"Northeast corner. We exposed it an hour ago and called it in. Federal offense to touch it once you uncover it.

That would put us out of business pronto. We would be responsible and so would you, by the way."

The men walked across the site, keeping a distance from the excavation which was over twenty feet deep in places. Trout watched the edge of the hole, feeling light-headed and dizzy. Not far from the water's edge, the superintendent dropped a ladder and he and Trout descended into the excavation. The superintendent grimaced at Trout's shiny brown loafers. Trout missed the last rung and landed awkwardly.

"Where? I don't see anything," Trout demanded.

"Right there. That's a human bone. A femur I think, but I don't really know."

"You called it in to who?"

"State archeologist. It's required."

"You didn't think to call me first? Who's pays you? I do."

"Like I said, it's not up for debate. You don't notify that office, your license is kaput. I have the name and number of who you need to reach."

"Couldn't you just have finished the work? It'll all get buried again anyway. We're so close. What if that's just a moose leg and we lose all this time?" Trout was desperate for options. His temperature was rising, dwelling only on the massive ramifications of delay, and the cataclysmic shock wave to the penurious partners of Odin Forward.

He would be sacrificed.

"This is Indian country, Trout. We've hit a few unknown burial sites now and again. You respect that if you want to build anything up here. Who do you think you are, anyway? Rules don't apply to the big Twin Cities money men?"

"I'm the guy who just stopped payment on your check. You're off the job," Trout shouted and climbed the ladder aggressively, tossing it over when he reached the top.

Bill Trout sat in his BMW, assessing his next move, with his hands squeezing the life out of the padded steering wheel. *Why are people such compliant rule followers? Such suckers they are.* Everybody wants a job, but no one was willing to risk anything. He risked everything. He dialed the number the superintendent gave him and eventually reached a woman in the Minnesota State Archaeologist's office. She informed him that Ms. Miley was the one he needed to talk to, but she was on vacation for another week and not taking calls. In the meantime, she explained, all of the forms were available online to start a prereview process application. *A prereview process?* It sounded wrenchingly bureaucratic. Trout's Sturgeon Shores was on the verge of bleeding out, with an expensive two-acre hole sitting idle next to Lake Superior. Stockpiled dirt piles the size of Mayan temples guarded the excavation, but they were unprotected and susceptible to weather. The concrete footings and foundations were supposed to be poured and up to grade by Labor Day. This was all wrong, all wrong.

Back in his Duluth Hotel at Canal Park, Bill Trout plugged in a small printer and cracked open a large bottle of Grey Goose vodka. He poured himself a generous glass and dropped in a single ice cube. The printer began to hum and vibrate, and soon it spit out the first application form, followed by the second, then forty more pages of instructions, conditions, and warnings in red. He needed certified copies of land titles, site surveys, original topography, utility locations, the list went on and on. There was contact information for consultants that needed to be hired to accumulate findings in something called a Master Site Field Survey. The exposed remains must be examined and identified, ground penetrating radar was required to identify the extent and locations of any other remains. On top of all that, Odin Forward would need to pay for a ridiculously expensive 3D model of the areas deemed "archaeologically significant." Only then, after all of this specialized, costly work, would Bill Trout be told by bureaucrats where, precisely, Sturgeon Shores would be allowed to stand, if at all. It was a daunting obstacle, the likes of which he had never faced before.

Bill Trout downed a second glass of vodka and called

the office of his east-coast architect. He told them about the find, to stop the remaining design work and hold any unpaid bills. He perused photos of a happier day, scenes from the groundbreaking for Sturgeon Shores, one of him clasping hands with the nitwit Mayor Vernon Tung. How long, he wondered, until the first phone call from a reporter, or from Mayor Tung himself, who drove by the site daily? He needed to prepare a contrived response, written out in advance and carefully worded, but now after vodka that would have to wait for morning. The sun slipped behind the high bluffs of Duluth and Canal Park fell into shadows. Maybe it was time to turn up the heat on the acquisition of Palisade Point, Trout reasoned. It could be the silver lining he needed to assuage impatient partners. Odin Forward.

TWENTY-NINE

Palisade Point was drying out. The gravel drive still needed work and had some stubborn ruts to smooth out. I wasn't getting anywhere with just a rake, so I retreated to the garage to look for some other tool. It would be like Ed Martini to have some contraption buried in the recesses of the garage that was rigged for this very purpose, maybe a blade attachment for the John Deere. First, I wanted to top off the Camry, so I headed south on sixty-one to my favorite two-pump gas station. The day promised sun, and that was a welcome development. I could see the manager through the window, parked on a stool behind the cash register with a newspaper in front of him. I listened to the gas slowly swishing and spurting its way into my tank from the cracked hose. The rolling numbers on the pump slowed to a crawl and then stopped altogether. The pump wheezed. We were full.

"What's the news today?" I came through the door in

a good mood, setting off a dangling strap of silver bells. He looked up at the bells with a scowl. "I said what's in the news today?"

"Horseshit start to the weekend is about all. What a washout." The manager peered at me over his newspaper.

"Looks like the big project across the way is taking a break," I said, gesturing toward the future Sturgeon Shores resort.

"They were working last week and then pulled all the equipment off. I don't know what's going on over there. It's an awful big hole in the ground—that much I can tell you," he said, snapping his newspaper.

I wandered through the cluttered and claustrophobic store, checking out the merchandise, when a group of three boys, all about the same age, maybe nine or ten, burst through the door, igniting the bells again. They seemed to be arguing over candy, and one waved a five-dollar bill over his head with a devilish grin. They settled in at the candy rack, still arguing on what to buy. I examined a boxy concrete tank filled with anxious gray minnows. They were darting from corner to corner in a hypnotic murmuration. *I wonder if these minnows have any comprehension that they are right next to the greatest body of fresh water in the world?* I doubted it. But it would be tantamount to hearing that God was in the next room waiting for me. The little minnows trusted in their habitat, the concrete walls of their universe, and were in a blissful peace, it seemed to me. Watching them in their world, it occurred to me that I had, at some point, given up thinking ahead to life after Palisade Point. Every day I seemed to slather another thin layer of varnish on the pretension that I was home, after all these years of living my vagabond life. I knew it wasn't true.

There was a sudden notion swimming in my brain that my biological parents had passed by this modest gas station, with its two decrepit pumps. They had, however briefly, occupied the space here. We existed in the same space, separated only by time. I conjured an image of them, fuzzy and faceless, my father leaning against the car door, waiting for the tank to fill. My mother in the passenger seat checking her lipstick in the mirror. I focused on the make and model of their car, but those details were stubborn. It was rust-colored, but then it all washed away, and I was back looking at the minnows. The hazy picture came and went in a breath, but they looked young and happy, with no hint of despair about their abandoned son.

It was still too soggy to do much outdoors, so I decided to drive to the Temperance River and follow one of the winding trails down to Superior's edge. Most people seem to prefer hiking upland from there, hiking up the Sawtooth Mountains to take in the glorious views amidst the towering waterfalls. I felt a tug instead to the big water, where the crashing surf elevated your heart rate. There were a handful of trail openings in the brush along Highway 61. I knew that each trail wandered differently and offered a unique experience, so I looked them over and made my choice. I picked the narrowest one that was a bit overgrown, thinking it was not popular. The path followed alongside a burbling tributary that spilled down toward Superior. There were short stretches that were hazardous enough to have wooden railings. The roaring falls high up in the Sawtooth Mountains were reduced to a distant hum down here, mostly obscured by the crashing surf. As I stepped cautiously toward the big water, the air turned cool and wet. I could see the exploding white caps through the leafy thicket. They swatted the shore and sent round stones airborne.

I went off-trail and climbed down a series of craggy rocks, unsure of my footing but too late now. Safely down at the water's edge, I settled in between two gargantuan volcanic rocks that stood sentinel on either side of a twenty-foot-wide gap filled with a million polished stones. It was littered with bare sticks and sun-dried seaweed. I planted myself in the warm stones that basked in the midmorning sun. At this proximity, there was no cause to mark time in the presence of Superior. The sun hung in the eastern sky. For the moment, the Earth seemed without people. I sensed only the power and equilibrium of the big water. I resided in the temple of the most sacred. In *The Lonely Land*, Sigurd Olson described "that intangible sense of remoteness and solitude that comes only from inaccessibility." The curling green waves swelled and released, swelled and released, swelled and released, in a timeless and divine dance, all for one lone observer.

THIRTY

I awoke in darkness, and the glowing digits on my clock confirmed it was an hour until daybreak. A flickering dream vignette lingered into waking; it must have followed me back to the real world, and it clung to my shadowy bedroom ceiling. I was three years old, wearing leopard-print pajamas and sitting on the living room floor in front of a small television set tuned to some police drama that I didn't understand. I held a small bowl of vanilla ice cream with rivulets of crème de menthe sliding down the sides. It was nestled on my lap, and I spooned it into my mouth a little too quickly and gave myself a headache shock. There was a man resting, relaxed in a stuffed recliner next to me, eating ice cream from a larger bowl. He casually glanced over at me, held up his spoon, and winked. His eyes and mouth were so familiar that I knew this was my real father. It was an untrustworthy recollection. I did not remember my real father, but the one in my dream visited me sometimes and made me wonder if there was any truth to it. I heard a muffled snort come from Ann's room and the scene on my ceiling retreated back to where it came from.

Ann's phone rang unexpectedly; it made me jump. After a few rings she finally picked up and there was silence followed by several rapid-fire exclamations from Ann. It had to do with Ed Martini and I feared the worst. Not knowing what else to do, I snapped on the lamp, put on pants and a shirt, and quickly brushed my teeth. Ann burst in without knocking. She looked confused and was clapping her hands.

"Can you take me to Duluth? Dad's not well."

"What's happening?"

"Caprice called and Roxie's with Dad at Hearthstone."

"We can go now, Ann. Whenever you're ready."

Ann went back to her room to get dressed and was at the front door in five minutes, holding a full box of tissues. I tried and failed to make coffee in time, so would do without. My head was still groggy, but I expected to sort myself out on the road. I was thankful that the Camry had a full tank of gas and thought again of the slow-turning numbers on the gas pumps in Schroeder. There were few cars on Highway 61, and the road was eerily illuminated by a waxing gibbous moon in a cloudless sky near the break of dawn.

"Caprice convinced Roxie to spend the night with Dad at Hearthstone and Roxie agreed. She called Caprice late last night and said he was asleep but losing his color with blotches on his fingers and toes. An hour ago, he was breathing erratically and Hearthstone told Roxie to call." Ann was wiping away tears with a tissue, staring straight ahead, taking deep breaths and blowing them back out.

I didn't expect any patrols out this early, so I got it up to seventy, about as fast as I could handle on North Shore Drive in the predawn. Ann anxiously slapped the dashboard when we hit a red light in Two Harbors. By the time we arrived at Hearthstone, Caprice was waiting for us inside the glass vestibule. The door locked from the inside during off hours. She let us in, hugged Ann, rubbed her back, and kissed her on the forehead. I thought of the day Ann first brought me to Hearthstone to meet her father. Ed had touched me on the chest with a knot of knuckles, his sincere brown eyes had smoky rings around the irises. I got his message loud and clear. He silently implored me to guard his treasure, his daughters. He might have believed that I was his last resource. He was a seriously diminished man and his most precious possessions in the world—Ann and Roxie—were well beyond his paternal reach. Caprice locked arms with Ann and started down the corridor while I stayed back in the empty lobby out of respect. I felt an ache under my sternum where Ed Martini had touched me.

I wandered the lobby for what seemed like hours, but it was probably minutes. The room faced east and gradually filled with light as the day shift arrived and the distressing silence was mercifully lifted by human voices chattering about routine things. I made my way over to a table in the corner and sat down. A few magazines were stacked on an adjacent credenza. I leafed through them until one caught my attention halfway through. It was an article about steam locomotives. I mostly looked at the photos since my eyes refused to focus without coffee. The piece was about the vast collection of historic locomotives housed at Duluth's Depot Museum. A picture of a metal shield mounted on the front of a locomotive was referred to as a "Cow Catcher," and that thought made me stand up and look outside. I turned around to see Ann in the lobby.

"Owen, come and see Dad." Ann was frightened.

"Are you sure you want me in there?" I responded tenderly, tentatively, and also with tingling trepidation because I had never been in the same room with impending death. I wasn't prepared to look it in the eye. And I didn't want to make matters worse with an ill-fitting or plainly ignorant statement. I took Ann's hand and we walked down the ghastly bright hall. There was audible groaning coming from the open rooms.

I followed Ann into Ed Martini's room, taking care not to bump into anything. His hospital bed had been moved to the far side of the room, away from its view of Lake Superior. There, a makeshift pharmacy counter and a collection of whirring medical equipment was set up next to his bed. I wondered how long Ed Martini had been deprived of his view of the lift bridge, but it no longer mattered. Roxie got up from her bedside chair to hug me weakly. She whispered something about Ann in my ear that I didn't quite catch, but I pretended to understand. Her face was swollen, and her eyes seemed smaller, and dark.

The Martini sisters and Caprice Wind moved around his bed, stroking his ashen face adoringly and taking turns caressing his hand. This was no longer the Ed Martini I had met recently for the first time. His eyes were crusted shut. His mouth was dry and hung open. Roxie dutifully applied lip balm. He was motionless, except for his bony chest, working hard for the air that barely inflated him. He was a helpless baby robin, still blind in the nest, beak open, begging for a morsel of food from its mother. His temples and forehead were jaundiced. The girls were telling childhood stories and I wondered how this was possible in the moment. My inexperience and ineptitude were unbearable. Maybe this was a Godly moment for siblings, the reason they were created in the first place, joined together for a goodbye to their beloved father, who was the source of their biology and their spirit. Not being overly religious, it was still easy for me to feel Marie Martini's presence next to Ed, watching and waiting. I stood stoically, wishing only to be invisible.

A nurse's aide entered the room and whispered something to Roxie and Ann, and they both nodded in agreement. The aide filled a syringe with a brown liquid and injected it into Ed Martini's arm, which was mottled and bruised. Almost instantly his breathing was less desperate but shallower. Ann and Roxie held each other alongside Ed Martini, and Caprice sat on the foot of the bed. I decided to slowly back away, and I returned to the lobby, where the morning sunshine had turned everything a pleasant pink. A new receptionist had arrived and was unpacking a very large purse. She put out a new magazine on the table, *Scientific American*, and I was quick to pick it up, and grateful for a distraction. My eyesight stabilized and I could read finally. There was coffee brewing somewhere, I could smell it.

After another two hours, I was hungry and chastised myself for such selfishness. Then Caprice peeked around the corner.

"Ed passed." She mouthed the words to me.

THIRTY-ONE

It was easy to see the instant relief on Ann's face when she hung up the phone. Her mother Marie's youngest sister Arvonne Jacobson—Aunt Arvonne—had insisted on making all arrangements for Ed Martini's funeral in Hoyt Lakes, if Ann and Roxie agreed, which they did immediately. Roxie brought up the fact that they hadn't spoken to Arvonne since Marie's funeral six years ago, and there was a tinge of guilt in her voice, but it was immaterial in the moment. They were both simply grateful. The sisters traded stories about their first spring at Palisade Point, back when Arvonne and her husband Neal Jacobson spent weekends at the resort helping Ed and Marie with repairs and clean-up. Roxie said Aunt Arvonne was extremely proud of the fact that her maiden name remained the same after her marriage: Jacobson. The families did some exploratory genealogical research for safety's sake, just in case, since the Iron Range was a fairly closed community where most were related to some degree. "They were so young back then," Ann muttered, studying a picture with a doleful look.

"Mom and Dad were kids with a new toy when they bought Palisade," Roxie observed, laying out a stack of photos, then taking a break to rub Ann's shoulders. Ann flipped through an untied bundle of old Christmas cards on her lap.

"Aunt Arvonne never missed a year, but we've never sent out anything at Christmas." Ann opened one of the cards, and I could see the blue writing inside. She handed it over to Roxie. Ann told me that Arvonne Jacobson had lived her entire life in Hoyt Lakes, marrying Neal Jacobson when she was just nineteen. He was ten years older than she was. Ann described Arvonne's lifelong affection for Our Lady of Lourdes Catholic Church, where she and Neal were married, and where Marie's funeral was conducted, and now, Ed's too.

On the day of the funeral, Caprice drove Roxie to Hoyt Lakes in Roxie's VW, and I took Ann in my Camry, after vacuuming it thoroughly and wiping down the dash. I wasn't familiar with the way to Hoyt Lakes, so I asked to follow and Roxie warned me to keep up. Hoyt Lakes was fifty miles inland from Superior, nearly due west of Palisade Point, but Caprice said that the best route was south to Silver Bay, then back northwest to Hoyt Lakes. It would be about a ninety-minute trek under sunny skies with stringy filaments of white clouds festooned overhead like bunting.

When we arrived at Our Lady of Lourdes, I got my first look at the Martini sisters together in their funeral attire. They strolled toward the church arm-in-arm. They both wore long black dresses, close-fitted, with diaphanous sleeves that appeared too delicate to touch, like insect wings. I had the sudden idea they were instead two lovely Parisian women on a lazy shopping spree with time on their hands. That was a ridiculous thought that I chalked up to my general misgivings about churches. Caprice followed them like a factotum in a dark blue suit with a black necktie. Carillon bells rang out, leaving behind mournful echoes in the summer air.

Our Lady of Lourdes had a modest cemetery on a low grassy knoll on the east side of the church. A burgundy canopy had been erected over an open grave, and a large mound of dirt nearby was loosely covered by a green carpet. When the Martini sisters disappeared through the church's door, I turned my attention to the curious device at the grave. It was constructed of a chrome metal frame with wide woven straps. I hadn't seen anything like it before and concluded it was designed to facilitate a casket's respectful descent into the ground. I had no experience with funerals and had only been inside a church a few times when I was child, during one of my early placements, I think, in tiny Mercer, Minnesota. It was Episcopalian, I remembered, because as a boy the word sounded more like a disease to be suffered than a denomination and it stuck with me.

I made my way inside and was instantly met with an invisible curtain of fragrant flowers, lilies and magnolias. The aroma was imbued with a decayed quality that I didn't care for. Further ahead, Arvonne Jacobson was sympathetically guiding Roxie and Ann into a small side chapel with massive doors made of carved wood panels and beveled glass. Caprice followed them inside, and I waited in the lobby, although I knew there was a special name for it. I could see at least nine or ten people gathered in the side chapel, well-dressed for the occasion. They traded embraces and milled about examining photos mounted on boards. I thought it best to proceed to the sanctuary, where the booming organ had started playing slow, somber dirges. The big room was tall and narrow, with intricately segmented colored glass filling up the vertical gothic openings. Streams of light danced against stucco walls and bathed the space in warm colors. Slender ivory candles stood on either end of a long oak altar that was draped with a white cloth in the middle with sparkling gold embellishments. A few people were already seated in the pews, and some knelt with folded hands. It was an otherworldly spectacle that made my stomach churn like I was an interloper, uninitiated and uninvited. I slid into the last row and pretended to concentrate on a brown hymnal. It had thin pages that smelled musty, but not unpleasantly so. It brought to mind Gideon's wonderful bookstore.

"Owen," a man whispered from my left side.

I turned to see Dean Aker, my jovial bartender friend from the Blue Heron. He was so far out of his normal context that I had a delayed recognition that must have seemed rude. Finally, I smiled back and we shook hands. Then I remembered a clue from our very first conversation at the Heron. Dean Aker knew Ed Martini years ago, when they had worked together in the trades. I was frankly relieved to see him and patted his shoulder.

"I certainly didn't expect to know anybody here. I'm a little out of my element."

"I try to make them all since I took the cure. Our whole generation is starting to die off. Ed Martini. So sad his last years were that way. When I tip over there probably won't be anybody left to come to my funeral. That's the way it goes, I suppose. Better to be seen than viewed, right? I'm here now. And so are you. How are Ed's girls?"

"Seem to be holding up," I said. "Wasn't a total surprise, you know, with his condition, but I could tell that Ed still being alive kept them connected. They visited with him. Ann said that even though you know it's coming, when it happens the world goes gray."

"Very true, very true," Dean Aker whispered upward, twisting his snug wedding ring.

"They have family here in Hoyt Lakes, on Marie's side. Their Aunt Arvonne."

"There is no substitute for family."

I felt an immediate need to change the subject. I looked back to see the chapel doors still closed and caught a quick glimpse of Roxie hugging Ann.

"Dean, have you heard what happened at Sturgeon Shores? Why the shut down?"

Dean shook his head and furrowed his brow. "They had a Bobcat hook into some Indian remains. Burial site."

"Ojibwe?" I asked, slightly boastful, knowing that it was the region's predominant tribe.

Dean shook his head again. "Nope, Cree."

"Cree? I never knew Cree Indians were on Superior." I had a working knowledge of North American tribes and had always associated the Cree with south central Canada. The organ moaned to a stop and church fell eerily silent. Dust was caught up in the colorful light rays.

"That's the problem," Dean whispered. "The Cree migrated north to Hudson Bay five hundred years ago. The burial site is ancient. It's got everybody up in arms. Tribal governments, archaeologists, politicians. That project will be stalled for a very long time."

The organ resumed with a full-throated, triumphant fanfare, as men in black suits wheeled in a copper-colored metallic casket with polished handles, followed by a queue of clergy in white and green vestments. Behind them trailed Roxie and Ann holding onto each other, with Aunt Arvonne and Caprice next and then other family. I observed the ritual with curiosity and apprehension: the memorized language, the recited creeds, and the incomprehensible hand gestures around the altar. The lead priest asked everyone to be seated. I could see Ann's head resting on Roxie's shoulder. The printed bulletin shared that the lilies and magnolias were a Martini family tradition and had adorned the church during the marriage ceremony of Ed Martini and Marie Jacobson. They were generously provided by Arvonne Jacobson.

After two hymns, the priest behind the altar slowly rose from his chair and ascended the pulpit. After a long pause, he began to share a story about Ed and Marie Martini. He told of the pure joy of knowing them both for many years, long before their big move to the North Shore. Ed loved and respected his Lord. Bible readings followed, first a poetic piece from Psalms about being lost but not alone, and then a message of hope and blessing from the Book of John. I had never read the Bible but these were wise narratives. The priest was a confident speaker: self-assured, but humble, with a vocal cadence that held my attention. The altar candles added a sense of mystery, like those in Ann's bedroom. Then Caprice Wind was invited to take the pulpit in her crisp blue suit and black tie. Her long black hair fell across her shoulders.

"My name is Caprice Wind and I am a special friend of Roxie Martini. When I was ten years old, my great-uncle Donald told my father that he wanted to understand the big water, which was Lake Superior. My father was upset about this because Uncle Donald sometimes got angry for no reason and did strange things that were also dangerous. One day, Uncle Donald took a rowboat out into Superior and just kept rowing until he was out of sight from the shore. My father was saddened by this, and after two days he told everyone that Uncle Donald was drowned in Superior. The next day, Donald was picked up by an ore boat after he drifted into the shipping lanes. Uncle Donald never spoke about what he learned so far out on the big water, but everybody said that he was different after that. He was peaceful and happy and not angry anymore, even when he got sick, but he never talked about it. I think that's why Ed Martini came to the big water. He wanted to hear what it had to say, too."

Caprice returned to the first pew and sat down next to Roxie and draped her arm around her subtly bobbing shoulders.

I sat solemnly behind the wheel in the Camry while the relatives and friends walked together in pairs behind the wheeled casket along a narrow path to the grassy rise. I was reluctant to intrude on the burial, so my car seemed a sanctuary where I could safely observe. The permanence of burial gnawed my gut and I looked forward to closing my bedroom door for a while to recover my balance. Ed Martini was sealed inside that metal box forever with no possible escape. I rolled down the window to lighten my sudden claustrophobia. Ed's magnificent and talented hands mastered the construction of complicated and mundane things, things that functioned well and lasted, and his mind articulated a plan to find heaven on Earth with his beloved Marie along the shores of Lake Superior, and his body that stood for so long as the family's mainsail mast, lending support to everything it touched—all of it now was inside that box. The casket descended slowly and disappeared from my view. I longed for one lucid conversation with Ed Martini, a man who I thought of often over past months, about his quest for Palisade Point, bringing up his remarkable daughters, and what he had learned over the years from the big water. Just one conversation.

THIRTY-TWO

"Roxie didn't come back?" I asked Ann, stooping to peek out of the window.

"Caprice convinced her to stay in Duluth for a few days. I think that's a good thing. I knew she would take this harder than Mom's passing, and she dismisses any consolation from me. I don't have any energy left, Owen. It's all too depressing. I've canceled everyone for the weekend. They all understood and wished us the best, except for the Winkels. Betty Winkels was gruff with me, even after I explained, but I never liked that family anyway. She's a complainer always looking for a compensatory discount. I hated to have to do it—we need the money—but I'm pretty useless and I just don't want to talk, except maybe to you, Owen," Ann explained matter-of-factly while checking through her notes in the cabin registry.

"One weekend can't matter that much, can it?" I said,

searching Ann's face, looking for a crack in her iron facade. Nothing showed through as she diligently scribbled notes on a legal pad, stopping once to tap the pencil eraser against her forehead. I checked out the long looping driveway that finally appeared to be bone dry after the downpour of Fourth of July weekend.

Ann covered her mouth and tears erupted. "He's gone, Owen. I can hardly take it."

"Try not to think too much right now," I offered awkwardly. "I'm working on Four and Five this morning."

"I'm canceling them out for the season. I don't really want a reprise of Underdahl banging on our door at night in the rain. No thank you." Ann recovered and was businesslike, keeping her eyes on her work. She reached for the calculator.

There was a disconcerting blanket of despair strewn across the kitchen, and I was powerless to mollify the moment. I took out of the cupboard the familiar mug with the antler handle and filled it with coffee. On some level I prayed that Ed Martini's wisdom would flow out of the handle and wind its way up through my nervous system to trigger a constructive suggestion between my ears. But after two tentative sips, there was still nothing. Just birds, two tiny spotted Chickadees, hopped about in the deep grass outside our open window. Ann looked up to see me with her dad's favorite mug. She frowned at me. My mistake.

The drenching rains over the Fourth, besides rendering the driveway a rutted mess, had also left me with shin-high grass across the resort with white patches of skinny hatted mushrooms poking through. Mushrooms are like alien life forms that slumber underground waiting to be brought back to life by abundant water. I looked forward to cutting everything off nice and low to let the sunshine return things to order.

I thought it best to leave Ann to her cancellations, so I wandered down to the big garage. I was motivated to explore more of its tantalizing contents, and to remember Ed Martini. There were still dozens of boxes and barrels I hadn't touched yet. It was, for me, a veritable treasure hunt, with hidden odds and ends that Ed Martini had at one time deemed valuable enough to tuck away. I went around to the back of the garage to tap on the red gas tank held aloft on its steel framework. Still half full, twenty to thirty gallons. A mismatched collection of wood planks leaned against the garage down at the far end. On closer inspection, behind them, I uncovered a tangle of rusted metal. I tossed aside several boards and tugged at the metal until it popped free and slid out in the open. I laid it down on the ground. It was an old metal box spring that had been modified with a heavy-gauge welded eyelet on one end. The metal springs had been cut out at the corners, leaving cavities that looked suspiciously sized for cinder blocks. Not so coincidentally, there was a stack of four cinder blocks stacked neatly nearby and it wasn't hard to see that they were meant to be dropped into the pockets created in the box spring. This was it. This was another one of Ed Martini's practical inventions, one designed specifically to smooth a gravel driveway after a torrential rainstorm.

I backed out the John Deere and fastened a chain to the hitch. I dragged the box spring around to the front, connecting it to a length of chain, about ten feet long. Then I loaded the box spring with the four concrete blocks, climbed aboard and dropped it into first gear to start out slow. When I got onto the gravel driveway, it was immediately apparent that the contraption worked like a charm. I made two clockwise passes, followed by another two in the opposite direction. The driveway was miraculously restored in a matter of an hour. I went back to my work bench and raised Ed Martini's favorite antler-handled coffee mug in a cold coffee toast to its inventor. His Titan Industries sign mounted on the garage wall almost seemed to smile.

The grounds were still soft in shaded spots, so I would give the mushrooms a stay of execution and wait one more dry day before mowing the grounds. I felt that Ann might prefer privacy, so I needed a plan. As much as I wanted to help ease her grief, I feared saying the wrong thing. I stopped to consider how I would mourn the loss of my own father, a man I had never met and whom I may not recognize if I passed him on the street. Worse, he would likely not recognize me. That situation delivered a hollow ache in my middle that pushed away the hunger pangs that started during my driveway repair. I opened the door to Number One and Ann hadn't budged from the table, still crossing things off her list and tapping away at the calculator.

"Still a little soggy to mow. I'll give it a day."

"Fine with me," she said stiffly.

"I'm thinking about heading up to Grand Marais. There's a trail head I'd like to check out. Any interest? It's going to be a perfect day."

"No. I have work to do here. You go. I don't mind. Really. I'm okay."

"Are you sure? Okay being by yourself for a while?"

"I don't mind. We could use some butter and coffee if you remember. Unsalted butter and dark roast."

I was instantly encouraged by the simple word *butter*. Ann was in no immediate existential peril if she wanted me to buy butter. My nagging apprehension of leaving her alone drained away, much to my relief. "I'll remember."

"Owen?"

I raised my eyebrows, listening closely.

"The driveway looks perfect. I watched you work. You found Dad's sled."

I was buoyed by the compliment and smiled back at Ann. "Around here there seems to be a tool for every problem if you look hard enough."

"I hope you're right Owen, I don't know," Ann said, looking back at her work. "You went the right speed. If you go too fast the sled bounces up and down and it doesn't work. Roxie and I used to ride on it when we were little."

I tossed my Sigurd Olson book in the backseat of the Camry and headed in the direction of Grand Marais, not certain of my destination but confident that I would find a challenging climb somewhere along the way. At Lutsen, I was enticed to take the turn up the mountain to take a look at the ski resort and gondola ride that originated on top. Winding upward toward the peak, I started to see the dangling red boxes through the trees; they were floating to and from the mountain peak, suspended a hundred feet in the sky by a thin cable that looked like a thread at that distance. Rounding the final curve, there were groups of people gathered on the platform at the base of a hulking steel tower painted green. They waited their turn to load, reminding me of the excited families at the Blue Heron's balloon festival. Once the paused gondola was fully loaded, the door snapped shut, and away they went in a southwesterly direction. I parked the car. Far across the valley of velvet pine tips, the red boxes furthest from me were mere red specks against the sky. I imagined the lake views they must have out there. A marvel of engineering.

I poked around the shops that were open for business on the mountain top, mostly logoed apparel and gifts, and one toy store full of games and puzzles that had the young children buzzing outside the door. One family looked familiar. I meandered through the first shop, called The Sprinting Turtle. I came upon a candle holder that appealed to me. It was made from a rough-hewn pine board that retained some of its bark along the edges. It was stained a rich coffee color and finished with a flat varnish. It had four niches bored into the top that held ivory-colored votives in glass holders. They were vanilla scented. I bought it for Ann.

The plain woman behind the cash register was gray-haired and in her sixties. She was chatty and accommodating, like everyone else in the Northwoods who depended on tourists for income. I set the candle holder down on the counter and she went on about how she bought the same one the week before and her husband always complained when she brought things home from work. Now, though, he loves it, she said. Her candles were orange but otherwise it was the same, and now with my purchase the item was out of stock. She told me it was my lucky day and handed me my change. I asked her about any good trail-heads at the top of the mountain and she pointed out the window and said something about Lake Agnes and her brother-in-law. That was enough for me to go on, and I thanked her with a nod and took my candles to the car for safe-keeping. I tossed a blanket over the top to keep sun off the candles.

According to the map on the sign, the trail snaked northeast along the Poplar River and led to Lake Agnes, high above Superior. It looked to be about two and a half miles each way, and that was a perfect distance for the day, since I didn't want to leave Ann alone longer than that. The map also showed several outlooks that promised spectacular views in all directions. I decided it best to leave my Olson book, *The Lonely Land*, in the car with the candles. I bought a bottle of water and set off to discover Lake Agnes.

THIRTY-THREE

Bill Trout deliberately flagellated himself by slowing down next to the shuttered job site that was to be his crowning achievement in real estate development: a cash spigot cranked wide open to gush forever. Sturgeon Shores. After just three idle weeks, noxious weeds proclaimed nature's patient take back of the smoothed dirt contours. *Horror vacui.* Trout reluctantly guessed that half of the property had been cordoned off by state and federal archeologists. There were stakes and plastic ribbons fanning across the land. A mobile field office was sitting just outside the demarcated zone. It was a converted steel shipping container with a steel door, barred windows, and an air-conditioning unit. It was painted bright white with a green state of Minnesota shape on the door. In his mind's eye, Bill Trout was mindful of the artist's stunning rendering of the colossal resort. He pulled off to the side of the road to take stock of the catastrophe—the stranded investment by Odin Forward would be staggering, probably life-changing for him. As currently designed, half of the suites, the lakeside restaurant, and a good portion of the event center were caught behind enemy lines in a no-build zone. Trout fretted that even the cleverest redesign would fail to overcome such a draconian land taking. Any legal recourse was likely a pipe dream. A loud air horn screamed from a speeding semitrailer behind him. Trout panicked as the truck blew by, sending a colony of small pebbles into the side of his BMW. He cautiously pulled back onto the road, checking his mirrors twice.

Trout had returned to the North Shore the day before from his Minneapolis office, where he had earlier adjourned a tortuous meeting with his east-coast architectural team. Rough sketches and paper blanketed the boardroom table, and notes were tacked up on the walls with masking tape. The sketches had a panicky quality and lacked grace. After the architects departed for the airport, Bill Trout vowed to never forget the closing comment by the firm's managing principal at the end of the maddening design session.

Bill Trout pulled the man aside. "Look, this has to be solved. There's no other option here and I need your full focus, and your flexibility. We can't reduce the size of the complex or the business side doesn't work. You can't just arbitrarily scale it down. It won't work financially. We've made very clear commitments." Trout crumpled a sketch between his hands and tossed it aside. "I don't have much design fee left in the pro forma. You need to be invested in this too. Sturgeon Shores is your project as well as mine, don't forget that."

"Bill," the principal began sternly, with no trace of empathy or concern. "We are paid well for our architectural designs, and we are commissioned for our proven skills and reputation. None of our design services are in any way dependent upon construction."

"What are you telling me?"

"What I'm saying is, frankly, I don't care if any of our designs are ever built. We will be paid in full. There's less risk for the firm if they remain on paper forever. We don't work speculatively."

Trout was in free fall.

That last verbal exchange was seared into Trout's brain for all eternity. The impatient investors that comprised Odin Forward Properties didn't yet comprehend the true extent of the problem, but they would soon enough. The investors were now the proud owners of a thick and expensive roll of architectural drawings that could only be built in one's imagination. Trout focused on the road and kept on driving. He felt cornered and weak. All of his bold promises and avuncular assurances at the Morgenstern Golf and Country Club were swarming him like malignant spirits.

A new course of action was still murky, inchoate, struggling to take shape in his vodka-addled brain. He knew he couldn't deny the cold truth, the blunt-force trauma of the Cree burial ground discovery. He needed something positive to leaven the blow, to deflect anxiety and buy time. He needed to secure the Palisade Point acquisition to restore confidence in his group. He would convince Odin that the archaeological discovery was a common obstacle for major developments along the North Shore. It was solvable, procedural, and merely the price of doing business on Superior. Even better, if handled smartly, the restricted burial ground would add a cultural mystique to a reimagined Sturgeon Shores, with a sheen of historical gravitas. Trout kept going. The lobby bar could be adorned with Cree artwork and authentic artifacts. *Why shrink from such adversity when you can monetize it?* Bill Trout was restoring himself, degree by degree, constructing his defense.

He resolved to make an unauthorized offer to the Martini sisters for Palisade Point. He would increase the cash offer by 20 percent, but he would communicate an even higher sum to Odin Forward. They wouldn't like the news, but he would convince them to strike quickly. The difference between the offers he would pocket to pay for the architectural redesign. If the architects refused, he would find a new firm to take over. The vision for Sturgeon Shores was already established and approved, the pieces just needed to be rearranged around a new, more restricted footprint. Trout knew from experience that he would need two separate purchase agreements, one to share with Odin Forward and another for the actual acquisition. It was fraud, he knew, but he had successfully pulled similar maneuvers in the past, and speed was the key. In any case, it was unavoidable. When Sturgeon Shores turned its target profit, on schedule, all would be forgiven anyway. Trout pounded on the steering wheel of his speeding BMW and pressed the accelerator.

Bill Trout turned into Palisade Point and was emboldened by the lack of cars. The place was quiet, with one white-haired couple sipping coffee on a small patio. They watched him suspiciously as he approached Number One. He rapped steadily on Ann Martini's door until she opened it.

"Good day Ms. Martini. I have some exceptionally promising news for you. Is this a good time to talk?"

"I've been thinking you were due to drop by. Come on in, I made coffee."

Bill Trout hesitated. The gesture of hospitality was unexpected. Trout's nerves were jangled and his usually dependable confidence flagged. He could ill afford any sympathy at this stage. He took a chair and deliberately placed his leather satchel in front of him on the kitchen table. "Coffee would be fine."

"So?" Asked Ann.

"Where to begin?" Trout forced a crooked smile. "Odin Forward is in an unprecedented and generous mood with respect to Palisade Point. The investors have openly discussed how this acquisition affects your family's legacy and needs to respect and honor your parents and yourselves. We are committed to preserving the memory of this resort in some important way, although the details are yet to be determined. We want you and your sister to be a part of the process. They wanted me to convey this sentiment to you in a most personal way."

"That's very kind."

"Your neighbor down the road, the Blue Heron, our property, is shattering its own records for profits this summer. The investors feel it's the right time to share some of that bounty with the Martini family who, let's face it, were pioneers in making this shoreline what it is today."

"There's a certain element of bullshit in there, but keep talking anyway." Ann squinted back at Trout.

Bill Trout frowned and extracted a manila file that contained a written offer for Palisade Point.

"There are identical copies for both you and your sister. I'll leave them with you to look over. You may have questions, and I'm a phone call away, day or night. If you want a lawyer to review them, that's completely under-standable."

"You can count on that," Ann said, knowing they had never hired a lawyer and wouldn't know where to start. Ann opened the folder. There were so many legal-sounding words it forced her to close it up again.

"Bottom line, Ann. The cash offer went up twenty percent. It's well above the market for this property, even with the improvements you've made this summer. Plus, we understand there's a little matter of a septic failure. Those are expensive, so the timing of this offer is truly providential."

Ann felt exposed and spied upon. She bit the inside of her lip and tasted blood. Where was Owen? She needed him now. She flipped through the document, her palms moist with perspiration.

"Give us some time."

"Timing is becoming quite critical, so I have to ask for your decision by next week. Otherwise, we're moving on to the next option."

"I'll talk to Roxie. She's due back this weekend."

"Okay. Ann, one more thing. Am I imagining it, or is it unusually quiet at Palisade Point?"

Ann's face flushed and she turned away to stabilize herself. "You don't know this business. With this sunshine and cool breeze today, who wants to be cooped up inside a cabin? We're full. Everyone is out exploring or down by the water."

Trout smiled again. "That's makes perfect sense to me." He gathered his papers and leather bag and retreated to his BMW. Turning back, he said, "Take care of yourself Ann, and I look forward to hearing from you soon." Trout felt momentum tilt back in his favor.

THIRTY-FOUR

Lake Agnes was well worth the hike. The trails around the lake were primitive and challenging due to rocks and roots. I could feel the terrain's impact in my arches and calves. But it was also that satisfying reminder of physical exertion that I craved. Lake Agnes was pristine and calm, cloistered inside a tall forest at an elevation high above Superior. The lake mirrored the surrounding pines and maples that had just begun their colorful turn in the first days of August. I encountered a pair of female hikers from Madison, Wisconsin, who told me I needed to come back in September to see a leaf display unparalleled along the Superior Hiking Trail. I had no doubt that they were right based on the wide variety of mature trees rimming the lake. I found several connected paths to safely circumnavigate Lake Agnes, which was divided into two sections by a jutting, tree-covered peninsula. I forged overland out onto the wooded peninsula and spotted a smoke trail wafting upward out of the forest canopy. Someone's campfire. I made a promise to myself to return with a tent and sleeping bag for a night on the peninsula's tip. I heard wolves by the lake, but they could have been coyotes since it was hard for me to tell the difference through the thick forest. I was tired and content once I wound my way back from Lake Agnes to Lutsen mountain and found my trusty (and rusty) Camry waiting for me patiently in the late afternoon with long shadows.

Palisade Point was quiet and still, much like when I left. The only sounds were vehicles racing up and down North Shore Drive to destinations other than our resort. The shades were drawn in Number One, and I pictured Ann napping. She hadn't been sleeping soundly since the funeral. Roxie's VW was next to Number Eleven and she was out on her new deck with a glass of wine. I got out of my car and shut the door firmly enough to get her attention. She waved me over with minimal enthusiasm. Even with a rather somber expression, her natural beauty and the symmetry of features were striking to me. Her long black braid was draped across one shoulder and resting against her crimson blouse. She wore a thick turquoise and silver bracelet that I knew had been a birthday gift from Caprice Wind.

"You're back early," I said warily, uncertain of her disposition.

"I had to come back sometime. Caprice wants me to

move to Duluth, but I don't belong there. Her family isn't too fond of me. She knows it, too, but keeps asking anyway."

"When did you get here?"

"About an hour ago. Look, Owen, I'm sorry I abandoned you two. I needed to think through things."

"We've been doing alright. We've had a few cancellations."

"Palisade Point hasn't looked this good since Dad was here, truthfully. Ann said you fixed the driveway with the sled. It works, doesn't it? We used to ride on top when we were little."

"Ann told me." I scanned the looping driveway with a sense of accomplishment. Roxie was more sedate and softer than I had ever seen; even her voice was changed, almost delicate. She appeared a bit dreamy.

"You know about the offer, Owen?"

"No," I said, but that wasn't entirely true.

"Ann got another offer from those Odin people. Odious is a better name for them. It's a lot of money. I'm thinking that Ann's right, that it might be time." Roxie gazed out over Superior, sipping her wine.

I was netted in a conversation that was far too raw and personal for my participation. A decision to sell Palisade Point was not a mere real estate transaction for the sisters; it was the abdication of a family's quest. An ending. I was relieved to see Roxie back home, though, for Ann's sake. I tried to redirect our conversation to safer territory. "Any cave tours this weekend?"

"We'll see. I pissed off a lot of people, canceling so many. I may start back up again, but if we sign the agreement, what's the point?" Roxie downed the last of her wine.

"I washed out the kayaks just in case."

Roxie looked at me silently. "Thank you, Owen. You've taken good care of my little sister. You're good for her and I was wrong about you." Roxie paused. "I miss my dad so damn much. I want to just listen to his voice in my head, and I'm terrified it will just disappear. I'll wake up one morning and it will all be gone, emptied out. I will call to him and hear nothing back. Do you think it's possible to forget someone's voice?"

"You can't forget your father's voice." I chose my words carefully.

Roxie left briefly and returned with a full glass of wine. "When I was thirteen, Dad gave me a tandem kayak for my birthday. A two-seater. He always expected me to teach Ann everything I knew about the world. He was so busy with the business. He never really said it directly, but things like that kayak were tough to misunderstand. I took her into the caves that first summer; she was in the front and I was behind her. We were barely out to sea when she exploded into tears, wailing until we were back on shore. She may have been too young for the caves, and I was older than my years and things didn't scare me. I should've known better."

"You were following your father's wishes."

Roxie gave me a nod and wiped a tear from the corner of her eye. "What do you have there?" She pointed her pinky finger at my book.

"A book I'm reading, almost done. It's called *The Lonely Land*."

"That sounds about right," Roxie said, holding up her glass to the light, bathing her face in amber light.

"I'll check on Ann."

Roxie smiled tightly.

I opened the screen door slowly to keep it from squeaking. Ann's door was shut tight, and I thought it best to tread lightly. I plopped into my favorite end of the sofa, kicked off my shoes, and opened *Lonely Land* at the last chapter. Author Olson, alongside his five best mates and the ghosts of the voyageurs who knew the water route well, were gearing up for the last leg of their five-hundred-mile canoe excursion in upper Saskatchewan, successfully navigating the treacherous Churchill and Sturgeon Weir rivers. He wrote in a way that suggested there wasn't any distance between the living men and the long-dead voyageurs. The living and dead were joined together at the souls, with a shared respect for the river. I had a tingling sensation that I should begin writing things down on paper, like my experience at Lake Agnes. It might matter to someone someday.

THIRTY-FIVE

I awoke with a heady rush of optimism that had no logical source other than a night of uninterrupted sleep and my favorite birds chirping at dawn. I usually woke when I heard Ann up and about in the middle of the night, so maybe she slept through, too. Ed Martini's passing marked the start of an agonizing stretch at Palisade Pointe, with Ann and Roxie grieving in their own ways. I tried my best to accommodate them both, mostly by listening. The life force had drained out of the resort and no amount of attention to the grounds seemed to resuscitate it, but I kept trying. With Roxie back home, Ann allowed herself a light moment and a laugh now and again, looking through photos, so maybe we were on the road to recovery on some level. We had been mostly sleeping apart these days, and I missed Ann dearly. I didn't bring it up and neither did she. Her room was perfectly still, so, stealthily, I made coffee and brought it with me to the garage, taking a lazy and circuitous route across the property. I came upon a patch of wildflowers that Ann said Marie planted back in the day. They were a happy jumble of color that I mowed around with care but never really examined. I liked to view Palisade Point from different perspectives, and at different times of the day. It was like a lake in that way: ever changing.

Circling back at last to my beloved garage, Ed Martini's erstwhile castle, I flipped on the lights above the workbench and admired for the hundredth time the Titan Industries sign mounted on the wall. It was Ed Martini's sign, of course, but I was seriously obligated to the stewardship of the porcelain and metal work of art. Glancing around, I noticed something new peeking out from behind a stack of wooden crates. I moved a few things to find Ed's original pencil sketches of the cabin layout. They were thumbtacked to studs in the far corner. My natural inclination toward preservation fired in my brain and I immediately considered that there must be a safer location for the drawings. These were as much a part of the resort's history as the Titan sign, and they deserved to be curated accordingly. The door slammed on Number Eleven and soon after there was Roxie, in a wet suit, striding up the rise toward Number One, to see Ann, who was probably still asleep. I was certain they had many things to share and plenty of baggage to unpack, so I was encouraged that their patterns of grief were to finally converge. I hoped for them both that the vicious sting of lost parents would eventually smooth into a milder ache. Chronic but manageable.

It was a perfect morning to cut the grass and I was looking forward to the relative normalcy of six cabins reserved for the weekend. While waiting for the sunshine to evaporate the dew, I popped off the blades and locked them into the bench vice for an expert sharpening. The aroma of grass cut with sharp blades was sweeter and more satisfying than chewing off the tips with dull blades. I reinstalled the blades, wiped down the John Deere with a soapy rag and polished the vinyl seat with a restorer that came in a tube that I purchased at the gas station. The John Deere looked brand new and maybe felt as optimistic as I did.

I finished the chore around lunchtime and was pleasantly surprised to see Ann and Roxie setting the picnic table with a sky-blue tablecloth, plates, and glasses. Ann gave me an exaggerated hand flourish, like a maestro, and I responded with a silly bow that I copied from a bellhop in an old movie I had seen back in Bayfield. I sat down, curious about the two hours they had spent together inside Number One, but that was for them to share, if at all. We had cold fried chicken, a steaming pot of baked beans, and a fresh Greek salad with the Kalamata olives that I developed a taste for over the summer. To me, it was a comforting and genteel feast that put us back to the start of it all. Ann and Roxie sat side-by-side, close together. A lilting collection of brass horns sang out from the screen door. Duke Ellington, I was informed.

In the early afternoon, guests began to trickle in, and Ann's Eskimo Pies made their first appearance in weeks. The day had gradually clouded over, so I checked the weather report and it looked like an evening squall line from the northeast would pass through quickly with wind and some rain, but the weekend promised warm August sun, a treat so late in the summer. The squall line never materialized and by dusk the three of us sat around a roaring fire sipping wine and enjoying the snap and hiss of newly split wood. Shrill voices in the distance, children laughing. It was a cool evening. I was pleased to see the same red oak fires dotted across the resort, releasing the inspiring fragrance of the Northwoods that we all shared. Later, when we ran ourselves out of wine, scattered raindrops made sizzling sounds against the hot coals. The girls got up simultaneously and I grabbed a miniature shovel to throw a few scoops of dirt on the fire while Roxie and Ann hugged and patted each other before turning in for the night. I swatted the steaming pile of dirt with the back of my shovel until I was sure that the buried coals were harmless. We were the last ones still outside.

I brushed my teeth and was elated to find Ann in my bed with the covers pulled up around her face. I turned out the light and we laid together for an hour or more before she fell asleep. I remained awake for a long time, content to stroke her soft hair as her head rested peacefully on my chest. Raindrops pinged against the window and the wind gusted with an occasional howl.

In the morning, the rain had stopped, but there was still gusty wind and Superior looked gray and choppy. I heard Ann in the kitchen, so I decided to shower before investigating breakfast. While tying my shoes I sniffed the air and knew there would be bacon.

"She signed it." Ann looked at me with a mix of astonishment and confusion.

"What?"

"The agreement with Odin. It was lying here on the table when I got up. Roxie signed it."

"And now you're not so sure?"

"I didn't think she would ever agree to sell Palisade Point. I never thought it would fall to me. I don't know what to do." Ann flipped over the agreement and stared out of the kitchen window at crashing surf.

"Maybe you should go down and talk to her."

"Owen, we're slowly going broke. I see it firsthand, every day, the hole we're in might look the same, but it's a little deeper every day, every year. So, it's a way out for us, at least, a way to set ourselves up for a future. I just never expected to have to face this decision. Roxie signed and it's all on me."

I sat down and looked at the agreement.

"Owen, I haven't paid you anything in weeks. The septic's shot. We've lost customers. I never pay bills on time. Why should this be so hard?"

"Palisade Point is part of your history, part of your family," I said, picturing Ed Martini in his hospital bed at Hearthstone. "All of your memories are here. Not many people can say they live as adults where their childhood memories were made. I can't. That's a very special gift." I was satisfied with my statement until recalling Roxie's poignant fear of losing memory of her father's voice. I was confused, too.

THIRTY-SIX

I finished breakfast and cleaned up the dishes, including the nine-inch cast iron skillet that had worked its magic on hickory-smoked bacon. The delectable odor of singed grease hung in the air, but figuring it might not be Ann's favorite, I opened two windows to get a cross breeze. The kitchen soon smelled of wet trees.

"She left." Ann came through the door said with a concerned look.

"Roxie? Where'd she go?" I nested clean dishes back inside the cupboard.

"I don't know. Her car's gone."

"Maybe Caprice?" I suggested.

"Maybe."

"She'll be back, don't worry. You two have a lot to discuss."

I started down to the garage to load up the pull wagon with another round of dry wood for the cabins. It was a gray start to the day, but already there was a brightness on the horizon. The tarp behind the garage was puddled with little cups of rainwater, so I carefully pulled it off the woodpile to protect the dry birch and oak underneath. I had more than enough split wood to finish out the summer. I already longed for the feel of an ax in my hands. I anticipated that Odin Properties might very well expect us off the premises before the end of high season. I wondered if I should ask to have a closer look at the agreement before she signed it. There was the thought of Ed Martini peering out at me from the gnarly thicket, demanding protection for his girls. I backed away from the wood pile to take a look around. Nothing. I decided to ask Ann.

Like all of his projects at Palisade Point, the big garage was built precisely. The sheet metal screws cementing the overlapping corrugated panels to the wooden structure were all evenly spaced at about six inches. Palisade Point had become, for me, in a span of months, more of a home than I had ever found, including the one glorious summer I spent on Miller's Lake. I worked my way around the building happily inspecting screws until it caught my eye. The yellow kayak was missing from the rack. It startled me in the same way a motionless snake in the weeds always did. A nauseating sourness struck my middle and roaring Superior went suddenly silent. Earlier there was concern in Ann's voice and I chose to dismiss it.

I found Ann in the kitchen, studying the agreement

from Odin Properties and making notes. Several pens were scattered across the table.

"Ann, I think Roxie took out a kayak. The yellow one's gone."

Ann stared straight ahead, wide-eyed, just as she had when the rampaging boulder tore across the resort, shearing off half of Roxie's cabin, Number Eleven.

"Alone? The lake is rough. I'm calling Caprice."

Ann shut her bedroom door and I could hear her excitedly talking with Caprice. There was a pause and then a frenzied mashing of words that convinced me that something was not right. I looked out at Superior and it had relaxed some, but still dangerously violent for a solo kayaker.

"Caprice is on her way," Ann said as she passed by me and pressed her face against the kitchen window. "Roxie shouldn't be out there alone. She knows better than to do that. See what I mean? She's so pig-headed. I can't count on her for any common sense. Now, I have to sit here and wait and stew until Caprice goes out after her. Damn it. I don't need this."

Caprice Wind pulled in at Palisade Point in a rusted Mazda spewing a trail of blue smoke. I didn't know she could drive. Ann was in the bathroom. I heard retching and the faucet come on, so I slipped outside to meet Caprice at the kayak rack.

"I don't know when she took off with the kayak, could have been early this morning," I shouted to Caprice half-way.

Caprice was solemn and deft as she tossed a blue kayak on the roof of her Mazda, snapping and tightening the straps that had vexed me last spring. "Her car is down at Tettegouche, so she's out. I drove right by it. She really shouldn't be out today alone. She's probably stuck in a cave. I'll find her, but we might have to wait out the wind to get back out."

I held the bow of the kayak while Caprice checked the connections. As soon as it was firmly mounted, Caprice jumped into the driver's seat.

"Be careful," I said.

"She must have needed solitude. There's no control over that."

The Mazda turned over after a couple of attempts and she backed out onto Highway 61 and drove south toward Tettegouche. She rounded the bend and disappeared be-hind the tall pines that lined the road. A gust of wind found a seam in the corrugated metal on the garage and whistled like a teapot.

Ann was still in the bathroom with the door open when I told her Caprice was on her way to Tettegouche with a kayak and that Roxie's car was there. We heard a screen door slam and a car start. The family staying in

Number Seven was leaving for the day and heading north. Yesterday they mentioned an early lunch in Grand Marais and maybe even all the way to Thunder Bay. Such joyous family plans were incompatible with Ann fidgeting by the window. Icy white caps relentlessly crashed against the rocky shore.

The morning dissolved into afternoon, and the weather grew mild with a hazy sun emerging. Ann was tense and not talking. I suggested we drive to Tettegouche to wait for them to come in. I reminded Ann that Caprice warned it could take a while to get back out of the caves in high waves. Ann agreed and grabbed a jacket.

"Okay, let's go," I said. "But, we should call the police before we go. If anybody's hurt, we may need help."

"We need police?" Ann was stricken by the suggestion.

"Only if we need help. That's all I'm saying. We have to get them both off the lake before dark."

"You call." Ann dug through drawers. She extracted a silver flashlight and an unopened pack of batteries.

I contacted the Cook County Sheriff's office in Grand Marais and gave them the situation. The man on the other end of the phone sounded concerned over the series of events. His voice became high-pitched when I added neither Roxie nor Caprice favored wearing life jackets. He quickly outlined the tactics for search and rescue on Superior that sounded highly professional to me. I wanted to correctly convey the tactics to Ann as best as I could. When I asked the man how long Roxie needed to be gone to be considered missing, he replied, "On Superior, missing is missing."

"What did they say?" Ann's voice was thin and raspy.

"They said we did the right thing to call because they mobilize immediately when someone could be in trouble on Superior. They already contacted the Coast Guard, the North Superior substation in Grand Marais. They dispatch a cutter that's docked there, a fast boat called *Decisive*."

"Oh, my God."

"I told them that she's probably in caves at Tettegouche. The cutter has two small motorboats on board and a helicopter that will sweep the shore. They bring divers too."

"Divers?" Ann screamed at me, apoplectic.

"They don't need divers, it's just a part of the response team," I countered quickly and immediately regretted mentioning the divers. I should have been capable of self-editing for Ann's sake, but too late. We jumped into the Camry and sped south. Five miles down the road an unseen helicopter swept by overhead with a vicious vibration that I felt in my lungs. I spotted the helicopter out over the water. It had a red cockpit and a white body that must be Coast Guard.

The two-row parking lot on the land side at Baptism River was occupied by just two cars parked side-by-side, Roxie's VW and Caprice's rusty Mazda. Caprice's blue kayak was still tethered to the roof of the Mazda and she was inside the car with her head resting against the steering wheel. Ann was animated and intense, rapping at the side window with her knuckles and bobbing her head back and forth to get Caprice's attention. I spotted the helicopter coming back our way. Something was very wrong. Caprice rolled down her window.

"Why aren't you out there looking for her?" Ann demanded, exasperated, breathless.

Caprice wiped her eyes. She was holding back tears.

"I have been thinking about things, Ann, I know where she is."

"Where?"

"If she's where I think, she's there by choice. She doesn't want to be found."

"Caprice! Goddamn it. Tell me where!" Ann howled and pounded her fists against the hood of the Mazda, leaving a dent.

"I love Roxie, Ann. But she's not coming back." Caprice uttered the words softly and then she rolled up the window and started her car. She backed out of the parking stall with Ann clinging alongside, slapping on the hood and shrieking for her to stop. Caprice sped away in the direction of Duluth, dark blue smoke trailing her car.

I managed to wrestle Ann back into the Camry, and she was nearly uncontrollable. Back at Palisade Point, Ann leaped into Number Eleven, and I followed her inside, unsure of what to do. She rifled through Roxie's kitchen drawers, then rapidly flipped through a stack of books on the counter. She spun around and darted into Roxie's room, where I heard clothes hangers jerked back and forth aggressively. It was then that I heard Ann drop to the floor and wail, a loud, guttural cry that sounded like an animal caught in a steel trap. My chest constricted. I found her in the corner of Roxie's bedroom, sitting on the floor with clothing strewn about. She raised her head to look at me.

"Owen," Ann said, struggling to speak, "Her wet suits are all still here. What does that mean?"

It was a terrifying recognition for me. I strung together the set of facts that, together, led me to a tragic outcome, one that hardly seemed possible even minutes before. Ann curled up into a ball and sobbed.

We returned to Tettegouche, not knowing what else to do. From the shore, we watched the cutter *Decisive* drop anchor two hundred yards out from the rocky cliffs in deep troughs. Uniformed figures dispatched two black-and-white inflatable boats with large outboards. They raced inland toward the shoreline caves, violently bouncing across the wave crests, with the motors yelping as the props came free of the cold water. The inflatables disappeared from our view, but we could hear still them. The helicopter hovered high above us, its rotor and ominous blades struggling to stay in place against a stiff wind from the east. Ann was ashen in my arms. The search went on for hours.

THIRTY-SEVEN

We huddled together on the couch, quietly, as the sun slid down behind the Sawtooth Mountains, momentarily casting the living room in a pleasing pale light, but it was short-lived and soon we were in shadows. The rising and setting sun were reminders that the world remained, and I hoped that Ann felt that way too. There was no way to assimilate the horrific day in any natural way. Ann was in a state of shocked limbo, next to me but wholly disconnected, a somnambulist, faraway in some dream. Did she wonder if time would ever start up again, or was she cursed to remain in this dreadful moment forever? I felt the warmth of her lithe body against mine and, so enjoying it, I felt guilty. It began to swirl in my head that my last conversation with Roxie, full of unlikely compliments for me, was her goodbye. I realized now that she had a plan. Roxie left the world on her own terms, shedding any last regrets with her restrained confession.

Roxie was gone, I knew, and so did Ann. I could see it on her. She gave herself over to the big water for reasons that drowned with her. Ed Martini might have done the same, given the opportunity, but one day he was rendered instantly helpless. Ann shifted her head to a pillow on my lap, and I was grateful that she moved. She stared into air. I thought again of Roxie, lifeless now in the deep depths of coal-black water, but still in our world, and not far from Palisade Point. I prayed that Ann was spared my disturbing vision. I stroked her hair, but she didn't react to my touch. I was not particularly religious, but I often sensed the mysteries of the universe. There was the welcome possibility that Roxie was now in the gentle embrace of her beloved parents, Ed and Marie. Darkness enveloped us and Ann fell asleep.

There was a soft rap on the door. I slid carefully out from under Ann to find two sheriff's deputies waiting outside. I remembered one of them from the day the boulder destroyed Roxie's cabin.

"Hello," I said in a hushed tone.

"Is Ann Martini available?" one asked.

"She's here but she can't talk now. She's sleeping. A very long day." I stepped outside into the night air, closing the door quietly behind me. I glimpsed Ann in my peripheral vision. "What can you tell us?"

The men explained that the Coast Guard called off activities for the night and would start up again at first light. We needed to be prepared that the rescue could soon turn to recovery. The helicopter had returned to Grand Marais and would not be needed again. It swept the coastline ten miles in either direction of Tettegouche. The teams on the inflatables had inspected all of the caves at Tettegouche and found no sign of Roxie or the yellow kayak. But sometimes lightweight craft are pulled out to sea by currents, or they can be shattered to pieces on the rocks. They had divers down in one of the largest caves, but the water was too deep and dark to afford much visibility, and jagged rocks made exploration highly dangerous in the dark. Then they told me something I already knew. Drowned bodies don't come up in the freezing waters of Superior, like they would in other lakes. In Superior they go down and stay down, preserved for eternity. For that reason, a recovery mission was unlikely to succeed, but best efforts would be made. The cutter *Decisive* was anchored overnight at Tettegouche. The officers apologized for our loss and offered to arrange a tow for Roxie's VW to the county impound lot in Two Harbors, if we preferred. I nodded approval. Ann wouldn't want to see the car at Palisade Point. They tipped their hats respectfully and left.

In the morning, I found a blunt note from Ann on the

refrigerator asking me to cancel the rest of the season's reservations. On the table was a stack of notecards with names, dates, and phone numbers. *Make up a reason*, she wrote. A message from Bill Trout was blinking on Ann's phone, so I switched it off and put it in a drawer. I gathered up the notecards, Ann's business folders and files, including a large spiral-bound calendar and headed to the garage to figure out the means and methods to shut down the resort for the remaining weeks of the high season.

I arranged everything neatly on the workbench. The material was all precisely annotated and cross-referenced to the master calendar. Ann's records were very clear and simple to comprehend. She even included bullet points documenting personal preferences, birthdays, anniversaries, and special requests. Her penmanship was artistic. I heard Ann approach behind me.

"Why are you all the way down here?" she asked with a swollen face and narrow eyes. Her hair was tousled and sticking up in the back.

"Saw your note and wanted to give you some privacy this morning."

"Forget the note and give all that back to me. I can do it. You shouldn't be the one. People are going to want to know what's happening."

"Maybe we should wait another day."

"I don't need another day."

Ann fell into my arms and clutched at my back with both hands. I felt her body lose energy, and I had the sense I was keeping her upright, a life-size marionette, unstrung. I kissed her sandy, disheveled hair that was damp with musky perspiration, and she nuzzled my chest. We stood there wrapped together, in the center of Ed Martini's garage, for a long time.

"Think about it, Owen," she whispered. "How do I lose my father, my sister, my home, my life, in one summer. How could God allow? What did I do?"

A tear fell into my shirt and slid down my breastbone. I was mindful of the confounding coexistence of Ann's fragility alongside her strength. She broke our embrace tenderly and touched my face with both hands. I followed her back to Number One, carrying along all of her materials. She stopped halfway to observe two squirrels chase each other around an oak tree. Later, I wandered the grounds, pondering Ann's misfortune. By noon the Coast Guard cutter approached from the south. They had given up.

That night in bed, Ann asked me to hold her as she slept. She wore a man's flannel pajamas covered with hearts, diamonds, spades, and clubs. I couldn't help but think they were Ed Martini's.

THIRTY-EIGHT

I had dropped off Ed Martini's sketches of Palisade Point at a frame shop in Tofte, and it was time to pick them up. One was a paper drawing of the original cabin layout when he and Marie closed on the resort, and the other an onion-skin sketch of Ed Martini's planned improvements, drawn shortly after taking over. Superimposed just right, together they formed an accurate depiction of the resulting resort. Frame-O-Rama's owner was a slight fellow with wild gray hair and spectacles at the end of his nose. He had been especially delighted to accept the assignment since he knew Ed and Marie Martini through the years. He had a genuine admiration for Palisade Point.

"So much of this kind of thing gets tossed," he said. "These drawings here, in Ed's own hand, these are real treasures, the ones we create for nobody but ourselves. You look at this and you can see the man's wheels turning. He was dreaming big back then, I remember, and it all began with these two drawings. Rest assured, I will treat them like they're part of the Dead Sea Scrolls."

He set out several frame samples on the counter. I asked about a blue mat the color of Superior on a cloudless summer day. I also wanted to make certain that Ed Martini's initials would not be obscured by the mat. Together we arrived at a simple black frame that would keep attention on the sketches themselves. I hoped it would become an heirloom for Ann, a physical memorial to temper the insidious disease of impermanence that took up occupancy in her house without her permission.

I didn't want to leave Ann alone too long, but since I was driving by the Blue Heron anyway, I thought it wouldn't hurt to stop and visit my bartender friend, Dean Aker. I wanted to inform him about the tragedy before the rumor mill started to churn. As usual, the lobby was brimming with activity, and hyper children darted back and forth through the gaps. They were understandingly oblivious to our situation. I worked my way over to Keegan's pub, but there wasn't even one seat available at the bar. Dean was nowhere to be found, so I tapped a young, redheaded bartender on the shoulder. He looked stressed and the perspiration on his pink forehead caught the lights.

"Where's Dean?"

"He retired last week," he said without looking up, counting out change for someone.

It was an abrupt proclamation and momentarily stunned me. Dean Aker seemed as rooted in Keegan's as the rock shelves lining Superior. Without Dean in the picture, the place was instantly reduced to an antiseptic kit of parts. There was no dancing bear gesticulating wildly behind the bar that gave the place a personality. I stepped cautiously back through the still-crowded lobby with the vague pinch of a friend's disloyalty, feeling that Dean Aker could've found a way to let me in on this, maybe even cautioned me against any budding friendship since he was soon on his way out. But, then again, maybe it had been a surprise to him, too. I hoped not. Either way, he was, for a while at least, my North Shore oracle and confidant. Now he was excised from my life without warning or apology.

Fortunately, Frame-O-Rama was still open but closing soon. I felt comfortable talking with the amiable gray-haired owner, and it was clear that he was serious about his craft, just like Ed Martini. He had the frame resting on a carpeted table waiting for my inspection. I could tell he was proud of his work. The mitered joints were flawless, the glass was pristine, the blue mat was Superior's best day, and the drawings were magically illuminated by their safe surroundings. We leaned in together to admire the work of two men, three if I counted for anything in the process. Ed Martini's earliest ideas for Palisade Point would eventually manifest into three dimensions and bestow upon the family a remarkable life. Ed's initials were respected by the framer and perfectly legible. I paid him in cash after he wrapped the jewel in two layers of brown paper.

I toted the artwork back to Palisade Point, resting it comfortably on the back seat of the Camry. My gas gauge dropped below the quarter mark and it made me consider my finances for the first time all summer. I was no longer flush with cash.

Ann was outside Number One when I got there. She was taking turns watering her petunias and pausing to snap off withered blooms. She patiently examined the flowers, and it was an encouraging development from my perspective. She gave me a somber but hopeful smile. I carefully extracted the package from the back seat of the Camry.

"What's that?"

"Wait until you see this, come on inside."

I positioned the wrapped frame upright on the couch and loosened the paper from the back so I could unveil the finished product in one smooth reveal. I lifted off the brown paper, and Ann's still-swollen eyes expanded. There was instant recognition. She got down on her knees and shuffled herself closer to the glass, circling each cabin with her fingertip, then tracing the long, looping drive-way. Ann leaned forward and softly kissed her father's initials.

"I think he always wanted to frame this himself, that's why he kept them. He just ran out of time," Ann said with tears welling in her eyes.

"It's yours now. Wherever you decide to go, you can take Palisade Point with you." A sharp pain buckled my chest and forced me to turn around and stare at the coffee pot. I got this one right.

"Will you hang it in my room?"

"Of course, I will."

THIRTY-NINE

By Labor Day I had grudgingly acclimated to a much more sedate Palisade Point. I knew that Ann was preparing herself to sign her name next to her sister's on the agreement with Odin Forward. She had read it through a dozen times, fretting over the language, rubbing her eyes. Bill Trout hounded her weekly, even with the knowledge that Roxie Martini was presumed deceased. He callously advised Ann to backdate her signature so that it aligned with Roxie's, which angered me, but Ann raised no objection. Trout capped off every phone call with the threat that Odin Forward was ready to pull the offer if it wasn't signed soon. Inevitability was in the air and strangely stoked my energies to keep up my now purposeless chores, perhaps a final act of reverence for a place that felt like home to me for the first time. A salute, of sorts, to Ed Martini.

I awoke early with the first morning light, and delightful birdsong swirled around Number One. I rolled over to find Ann wide awake, dreamily gazing up at the ceiling.

"Can I ask you something?" Ann said without breaking her trance.

"Hmm?"

"If I tear up the offer from Odin, would you stay here with me?"

"What?"

"If I tell Bill Trout to go screw himself, if I stay here until I either make it go or fail miserably, would you do it with me? Would you promise to stay at Palisade with me?"

Is this a serious idea? I lay on my back and joined her in ceiling gazing. Truthfully, there was no place on Earth I would rather be than alongside Ann Martini. That attraction had taken hold deep inside me by mid-summer, and I routinely ignored it for my own self-preservation. Now it screamed for articulation. I had considered it juvenile fantasy and probably disastrous. But now, in this shared bed, the thought of packing up and leaving Ann, of pushing off from Palisade Point for the last time, of losing another person in my life, of abandoning the garage shrine to my mentor Ed Martini, of never again playfully patting the prehistoric boulder that stood sentinel in front of Palisade Point, all of it, all of it gathered around me.

"Yes, Ann, I would stay with you, if that's what you want."

FORTY

The phone call to Bill Trout was mercifully short but only because Ann hung up on him. I could hear him shrieking expletives on the other end, and Ann held the phone away from her ear. "Think about it!" he wailed futilely at the end. Ann dismissively tossed the phone on the couch and pushed a red button on her stereo that let loose a favorite jazz number. She turned up the volume and began to move her hips rhythmically.

"Who's this now?" I asked, seeking the relief of a drop of joy in the air. I was eager to continue my months-long remedial education in the field of jazz music. I knew the main players, many of the song titles, and a few of the influences. It was a cultural cobweb.

"Cannonball Adderley. And that's his soprano saxophone," Ann added. "Not many can pull it off like he did."

I thought a saxophone was a saxophone, but there was still much to be learned.

I wandered outside to take stock of things and could

see Ann still dancing alone in the kitchen. If Palisade Point were to work as a viable business against behemoths like the Blue Heron, I knew changes had to be made. There were sizable holes to plug. I believed that Ann had, at least to some meaningful degree, anointed me her partner in life and business by asking me to stay. I had to take the chance that I could now make decisions too. We were in for the fight of our lives if we wanted to survive at Palisade Point.

I called Cook County later that morning and initiated the process for obtaining a septic installation permit. "You can start work without a permit," the man stated coldly, "but don't you dare backfill until the inspector signs off on the underground work. That would be your ass and mine." It was very good news. I ordered the delivery of a Bobcat from a dealer in Two Harbors that I would use to expose the piping to extend the drain field. Fortunately, there was plenty of open space around the failed underground tank. Doing some of the digging myself would cut costs by 20 percent, I figured, but I secretly worried I might gum up the warranty by touching the system. Cost wise, it was worth the risk. The other piece of good news from Cook County was that they didn't require the old concrete tank to be removed, so long as I cracked the bottom and filled it with sand. More savings. I had held an operator's license at one point in my so-called career and relished the opportunity to run a Bobcat again. It was incredibly satisfying to work the controls and move earth. I conjured the dashboard in my mind and, with eyes closed, I played with the invisible knobs until I had it mastered again. It was like riding a bike.

On Wednesday morning, the air turned dry and cool, an unmistakable signal, portending a dramatic weather shift. September had arrived on the North Shore, and there was no turning back. But it was the perfect temperature for the hot-motored Bobcat. The machine arrived on a flatbed trailer chained down to its moorings. Two young men in overalls pulled out a steel ramp from beneath the flatbed and loosened the tie-downs. One jumped into the cage and fired up the engine, and a blast of stinky gray smoke shot out of the front grill. He slowly crawled the snorting machine down the narrow ramp and into the grass. He handed me a card and told me to call if I had any trouble. I was supposed to let them know as soon as I was done with it. Ann was in the window and had stopped dancing. She looked perplexed.

Before I got underway, I called an outfit called Norman Septic in Hibbing. I had sent them pictures of the tank location, a view from the road, and the location of the cabins. I also told them to plan for at least three more cabins and to size accordingly. It was a straightforward job, according to the helpful general manager named Robbie. He liked the fact that his CAT excavator with its giant claw wouldn't have to account for any close structures or overhead power lines. "You should see some of the tight squeezes we've had to fit through. Last summer we hooked an electrical line and nearly killed everybody," he told me. The new concrete septic tank would arrive on a separate truck.

I quickly got comfortable with the Bobcat in my old ways, making some standard moves around the green expanse: turning, spinning, backing up, raising and dropping the bucket. After about thirty minutes of drilling, I was as ready as I could be. I started with the delicate task of scraping dirt to expose the drain field piping. It always reminded me of peeling the crust off a massive pie without touching the baked apples. By lunchtime, I had most of the first phase done, so I figured it was time to explain myself to Ann, who sat watching in the window and surely knew what I was up to.

"You're fixing the septic?" Ann asked apprehensively, sipping tea from her father's favorite mug with John Coltrane rolling softly in the background. I knew the song was "Stella by Starlight."

"Fix? Try replace. If we don't do it now, we can't get Four and Five back online by next season. Frost doesn't come out of the ground until May. That's no time for us to be torn up. And what happens when the rest of them go?

If we're in on Palisade, Ann, then we're in," I responded with the cool confidence I mustered when I was in complete control of a project. The new septic system was already designed and installed between my ears. I could visualize the whole project.

"How much?" Ann inquired reluctantly, smoothing her hand across her bound ledger.

"I have enough cash to cover the septic. But to be completely honest with you, there's not going to be much left over. We'll have to find our way through winter."

"Are you sure this is the right thing?" Ann watched the men working outside.

"I have never been this sure about anything in my life."

"Okay." Ann nodded.

"Ann, there's more to this plan. I have other ideas."

"What do you mean?"

"I'm oversizing the septic. There are perfect spots for three more cabins. There's room to do it and I can start accumulating the materials over the winter, look for bargains. We can build ourselves a coffee shop, too, with a deck and a perfect view of Superior. Big windows. Why should our guests have to go to the Blue Heron for coffee and muffins? Let's keep that money right here—and your muffins are better anyhow. People will love it. We'll cash flow the construction as we go, but I can do all the work myself. We can do this together. Really."

Ann rose, thoughtfully, gripping the mug with both hands, and she wandered ghost-like into her bedroom, where she paused in front the framed sketch of Palisade Point. I heard a sniffle, then she wiped her nose with her sleeve.

"So, about this coffee shop. Could we play jazz inside?"

"Why not? At the coffee shop over at the Blue Heron, all they play is Muzak versions of Madonna and Elton John that make me want to hurl. Our coffee shop will be known up and down the North Shore for its fine taste in jazz. Who wouldn't stop for coffee? We can put up black-and-white pictures of all your favorites. Frame-O-Rama will take care of it for us."

"They were all Dad's favorites. Maybe we can call it Ed and Marie's Coffee House?"

"Ah, now you're seeing it, Ann. We don't want to be another Blue Heron. We have a story that's real. Your family's history. Palisade Point has a story. With a future." I was energized by the thought and hoped that an adventurous banker from the Iron Range might soon become a trusted friend. That was a hunt for another day.

Ann rushed toward me and tossed her arms around my shoulders, kissing me on the lips and pulling us together. The Milky Way at night suddenly lodged itself in my mind. In daylight it was obscured by the veil of blue sky, but still it was there, watching, a fixture in the heavens, tugging us along inexorably on the wheel of its celestial vehicle. I could see Ed Martini wiping grease off his hands in the open garage door of his beloved garage, and there was Marie Martini kneeling in the green grass snipping the sour ends off the rhubarb stalks destined for sugar-soaked pie-making. And, further down the shore, Roxie Martini reclined in her ice water rock throne beneath the dark water. The columns of sunlight penetrating the cave were strong enough to illuminate the contours of her lovely face and her floating black braid.

"I need you, Owen."

"I love you, Ann."

EPILOGUE

Right on schedule, Norman Septic arrived midweek with a concrete tank loaded on one semitrailer, and the CAT excavator was on another. The crew was magnificently well-trained and hardly spoke; it was all simple hand gestures, and they moved about one another with practiced choreography. There was no fuzziness to the task at hand. The steel scoop was deployed and began grabbing at the earth with fury, depositing soil to the side pile with remarkable speed and precision. Down five or six feet, the new hole dwarfed the old exposed and failed tank, resting in the crater like a worn and scratched burial chamber, dead from so many years of service. The new tank was much larger and would soon take the place of its obsolete relative. The crew was finicky, working with the new piping and fittings, coercing and adjusting as they went along.

A Cook County pickup pulled in and I rightly assumed it was my permit delivery. It was the same inspector who intended to red tag our system until Roxie creatively put him off, and that was right before I unfortunately crushed his nose. The nose was still a bit off and he glowered at me with malice.

"You want to get out to take a closer look?" I asked him, feigning ignorance of his identity. He adjusted himself uneasily in the driver's seat and shook his head.

"I can see it from here. Take your permit." He held out a folded pink paper.

I snatched it out of his hand and the window started back up. He gave the crew a two-finger salute, and they returned it somewhat less respectfully. Ann and I set up folding chairs in front of Number One to watch the crew swing the hulking concrete tank over the deep excavation. It hung from four heavy-gauge chains attached to the raised bucket on the excavator. The operator inside the green glass cab was focused on the tenuous movements of the airborne tank, carefully avoiding any twisting of the chains. Slow and methodical seemed to be the order of the day once the tank was in the air. Ann brought out two glasses of Champagne, which I welcomed. The massive tank descended like a floating feather into the earth until it passed from our view. So did the crew, for that matter, who were all down in the hole making whatever connections were needed to enable our toilets to flush and our drains to drain forever.

"I can't believe you did this, Owen." Ann dropped her head in her hands. "Why isn't Roxie here? She deserves to be here. I don't understand. It's my fault."

"No, Ann, it's not."

"What if I had just torn up the offer on the spot?" Ann asked wistfully. "What if I never told Roxie? Would it have changed everything?"

"You did nothing wrong." I knew that was true. I gradually came to appreciate that Roxie experienced the world differently and she would leave it on her own terms, without any fears or regrets. Losing her father and Palisade Point left too big of a hole, and she gave herself to the big water to test her theories of God and the universe. She would have had no compunction about dancing beyond the cliff's edge. I got the feeling that my deep affection for her sister freed her from that one intractable responsibility of hers—protecting Ann.

The metallic clinking of steel shovels continued until the crew crawled back out of the hole. The big excavator blew steam and began depositing scoops of soil back right where they belonged.

Ann was pensive, sniffing the bubbles popping in her Champagne. "You know, Owen, I've been thinking about something else today."

"What's that?"

"Maybe if you stop moving around so much, just maybe your real family might find *you*."

"I'm not so much concerned about that anymore. I was, but not now."

Back inside, we set our glasses in the sink, and Ann turned on her music. Before long, there was soothing piano paired with steel brushes caressing a snare drum. She approached me to dance with her soft palms extended. We drew close together and began to sway to the pleasant melody, twirling slowly, back and forth in the safe sanctuary that was Number One. As the music receded into its natural decrescendo, I pulled back to see Ann's face. She was teary, yet smiling. I had never seen anything so beautiful in the world.

The end of September brought the first meaningful snow, capping the cabins in a thin white blanket that would last for a day, maybe two. Palisade's plumbing was running smoothly, with every cabin functioning like new. I seeded the topsoil over the new tank but did not expect germination in the fall. It was still worth the try. We were able to rebook six cabins for the weekend. I stopped for gas in Two Harbors and bought a newspaper, the *Two Harbors Weekly*. There was an article inside about Odin Forward Properties, and how it was preparing to auction its signature property, the mighty Blue Heron. It went on to say that Odin abandoned another project called Sturgeon

Shores in Schroeder due to extraordinary complications. It was halted by the discovery of an ancient Cree Indian burial site on the site's lakeside. Odin Forward was about to be legally dissolved, much to the chagrin of Schroeder Mayor Vernon Tung, who had been a tireless advocate for the Sturgeon Shores development. He called it a "dark day" for the town of Schroeder. There was a black-and-white photo of him in a plaid jacket holding a gold shovel at the groundbreaking for the project. It mentioned that a third resort, north, near Lutsen, never attained full entitlement and was consequently shelved. A footnote to the article stated that a former executive of Odin Forward, William Trout, had been indicted on a charge of fraud related to the financing of the North Shore developments and awaited trial.

My one glorious summer at the edge of Miller's Lake had planted a seed in a boy that led me back to the big water of Superior. I thought of the rickety mechanical funicular that carried me to the hilltop lair of the ancient coin collector John Chambers. I recalled peddling my bicycle so furiously that I expected to lift off the road when I crested the hill at the wagon wheel fence. I let go of the handlebars and extended my skinny arms out to each side. But now, here at Palisade Point, I discovered a new father who spoke to me without words, gifting me his wisdom, the fruits of his courage, and his rarest jewel, his Ann. It was an end to my peripatetic life, with my tools the only reminders of my many stops along the way. There were no guarantees, and risks abounded for Ann and me. But we were surrounded by the spirit of family and the sky turned blue.